Unbidden, a picture flashed before Nate's eyes of Brooke wearing her grandmother's wedding veil... wearing a lace gown...walking down the aisle of a church with a bouquet of flowers in her hands.

The idea startled him and he took a step back from the hope chest. Carefully Brooke folded the veil again and settled it in the chest once more.

When she straightened again, Nate was close enough to her to see the golden flecks in her brown eyes...to inhale her lovely scent...to read the longing on her face that he felt, too. This woman was too special, and he couldn't pretend they were strangers when they weren't. Yet he knew friendship with her could dangerously lead him into much more....

Dear Reader,

Now that the holidays are over, I'll bet you need some serious R and R, and what better way to escape the everyday and recharge your spirit than with Silhouette Romance? We'll take you on the rewarding, romantic journey from courtship to commitment!

This month you're in for some very special surprises! First, beloved Carolyn Zane returns with *The Cinderella Inheritance* (#1636), a tender, rollicking, triumphant rags-to-riches love story. Then Karen Rose Smith brings you the next installment in the amazing SOULMATES series. In *With One Touch* (#1638), Brooke Pennington can magically heal animals, but only Dr. Nate Stanton has the power to cure her own aching heart.

If the greatest lesson in life is love, then you won't want to miss these two Romance novels. In Susan Meier's *Baby on Board* (#1639), the first in her DAYCARE DADS miniseries, Caro Evans is hired to teach dark, guarded Max Riley how to care for his infant daughter—and how to love again. And in *The Prince's Tutor* (#1640) by Nicole Burnham, Amanda Hutton is used to instructing royal *children* about palace protocol, but not a full-grown playboy prince with other lessons in mind....

Appearances can be deceiving, especially in Cathie Linz's *Sleeping Beauty & the Marine* (#1637), about journalist Cassandra Jones who loses the glasses and colors her hair to find out if gentlemen prefer blondes, and hopes a certain marine captain doesn't! Then former bad-boy Matt Webster nearly goes bananas when he agrees to be the pretend fiancé of one irresistible virgin, in Shirley Jump's *The Virgin's Proposal* (#1641).

Next month, look for popular Romance author Carla Cassidy's 50th book, part of a duo called THE PREGNANCY TEST, about two women with two very different test results!

Happy reading!

Mary-Theresa Hussey

Mary-Theresa Hussey
Senior Editor

Please address questions and book requests to:
Silhouette Reader Service
U.S.: 3010 Walden Ave., P.O. Box 1325, Buffalo, NY 14269
Canadian: P.O. Box 609, Fort Erie, Ont. L2A 5X3

With One Touch

KAREN ROSE SMITH

SILHOUETTE *Romance*®

Published by Silhouette Books

America's Publisher of Contemporary Romance

With grateful remembrance of Anna Smith who gave Ebbie
to me, and to the Smith family for letting us adopt London.
To Andrea Bowman who enriches my path.
In appreciation of Sandy, Buffer, Cinnamon, Binky, Whiskey,
Mimi, Tam and Kasie who gave me years of
comfort, love and enjoyment.

 SILHOUETTE BOOKS

ISBN 0-373-19638-5

WITH ONE TOUCH

Copyright © 2003 by Karen Rose Smith

Printed in U.S.A.

Books by Karen Rose Smith

Silhouette Romance

*Adam's Vow #1075
*Always Daddy #1102
*Shane's Bride #1128
†Cowboy at the Wedding #1171
†Most Eligible Dad #1174
†A Groom and a Promise #1181
The Dad Who Saved
  Christmas #1267
‡Wealth, Power and a
  Proper Wife #1320
‡ Love, Honor and a
  Pregnant Bride #1326
‡Promises, Pumpkins and
  Prince Charming #1332

The Night Before Baby #1348
‡Wishes, Waltzes and a Storybook
  Wedding #1407
Just the Man She Needed #1434
Just the Husband She Chose #1455
Her Honor-Bound Lawman #1480
Be My Bride? #1492
Tall, Dark & True #1506
Her Tycoon Boss #1523
Doctor in Demand #1536
A Husband in Her Eyes #1577
The Marriage Clause #1591
Searching for Her Prince #1612
With One Touch #1638

Silhouette Special Edition

Abigail and Mistletoe #930
The Sheriff's Proposal #1074
His Little Girl's Laughter #1426

Silhouette Books

The Fortunes of Texas
Marry in Haste...

*Darling Daddies
†The Best Men
‡Do You Take This Stranger?

Previously published under the pseudonym Kari Sutherland

Silhouette Romance

Heartfire, Homefire #973

Silhouette Special Edition

Wish on the Moon #741

KAREN ROSE SMITH,

award-winning author of forty published romances, has loved animals all her life. She admits cats are her favorite. Her first cat, a yellow tabby named Sandy, allowed her to dress him in doll clothes and push him in a stroller!

Ebbie and London, the sweetest kittens on the planet, are her "babies" now. With her son being a graduate student in Tennessee, they have filled her empty nest. Happily married for thirty-one years, Karen Rose and her husband live in Pennsylvania.

Readers can write to her c/o Silhouette Books or e-mail her through her Web site at Karen@karenrosesmith.com.

Dear Reader,

This Silhouette Romance novel is close to my heart because I could combine the work I love with my love of animals. My heroine, Brooke, has a special affinity for all creatures. Her gift awes her and directs the course of her life. But in the past, it has also been an impediment to finding the love for which she's always searched. When Nate invites her to join his veterinary practice, he never expects to find a woman whose caring nature envelops him, too. As he fights the bonds growing between them, he learns the power of his love for Brooke can forge their future.

The idea for this story originated when my husband and I rescued a kitten from a friend's farm and nurtured her back to health. We later adopted her half sister, and they both bring me countless hours of joy. My hero and heroine find that same joy in the creatures they hold dear.

I hope this Silhouette Romance book touches my readers in a special way.

All my best,

Karen Rose Smith

Chapter One

She was starting over...again.

Brooke Pennington grabbed her denim satchel and looped the strap over her shoulder as she exited her van and closed the door. She'd have to take the van to a mechanic to get it checked. It was leaking fluid and coughing, but it had gotten her to Whisper Rock, Arizona, and she was so grateful for that.

Approaching Whisper Rock Veterinary Clinic, she saw it was a cedar-shingled building. Along one side she could catch a glimpse of the stairway leading to the second-floor apartment that Nate Stanton had told her was hers if she wanted it.

As early-January snow flurries began to swirl, she peered across the parking lot through the white flakes to a fenced-in front yard and a spanking-new, two-story house. A dormer above the small porch gave it a homey look. That house was Dr. Stanton's new home.

Home.

How she wished she could have one of those. But

wishes were less substantial than rumors, and twice over the past four years rumors about her methods of practicing veterinary medicine had forced her to pack up and find a new clinic where she could work.

Hopefully…

She took a deep breath of cold air, smiled up at the snow-filled clouds and resolutely opened the door to Whisper Rock Veterinary Clinic, hoping Dr. Stanton would be there—even though it was Thursday, his day off. She wasn't supposed to start until Monday, but she'd made good time driving from Syracuse.

A bell tinkled over the door when she opened it. Before she reached the long counter that divided the waiting area from the offices and exam rooms, a tall, ruggedly handsome man emerged from one of those offices, carrying a few files. On his heels was a black-and-tan German shepherd who stopped when the man did.

"Hi," Brooke said, her insides fluttering. "I'm Brooke Pennington, and I'm here to see Dr. Stanton."

The German shepherd trotted over to her. After a look into his eyes, she crouched down and petted him. "Hi, there. Aren't you handsome! Are you the welcome party?"

"That about sums it up," the tall man said, his voice deep. It resonated through Brooke as it had over the phone during her interview, and her gaze was drawn up to his.

The man nodded to the dog. "That's Frisco. I'm Nate Stanton. I didn't expect you until the weekend."

During the two phone conversations she'd had with Nate Stanton, Brooke had liked the sound of his voice and his take-charge attitude. She'd also liked his receptivity when she'd told him that she didn't want to become the partner his ad had asked for but rather an employee. He'd said that since he needed someone to share his practice immediately, he would accept that—and her—sight unseen.

Now he set the files on the counter and extended his hand. Drawn to him in spite of herself, she rose to her feet slowly, letting him grip her fingers. He had a large hand that went with his solid build—broad shoulders, trim waist, long legs. He was wearing a dark-green flannel shirt. His athletic shoes were worn and his jeans were well washed. He looked comfortable and masterful and downright...sexy.

Her tummy fluttered again and she managed to say, "It's good to meet you."

"You, too." His green gaze was examining her wavy, shoulder-length, dark-brown hair, her red-and-turquoise wool jacket, her black corduroy slacks and her ankle-high boots.

When Frisco bumped her hand with his head, she laughed. "I guess that's his way of introducing himself."

Nate nodded to the coffeepot on the back counter. "Would you like a cup of coffee before you get settled in?"

"I think I'd rather take a look around and get my bearings. I drove in last night and stayed at a motel at the edge of town. My suitcases are still there."

As his gaze passed over her again, less obviously this time, it was filled with masculine appraisal that brought color to her cheeks. "We can take a quick tour of the clinic," he suggested. "Or do you want to check out the apartment first to see if you like it? Maybe you've decided to stay somewhere else?"

"Oh, no. The apartment sounds perfect...and convenient."

He smiled easily, as if he did it often, as if he was confident and relaxed with his world. "Good. Then I won't have to worry about advertising for a renter. While we're looking around, keep in mind that partnership offer is still open." He studied her intently again. "I know we discussed salaried employment, but I've thought about it since our last conversation. Are you sure you wouldn't rather invest in your future, rather than punch a time clock?"

"There aren't time clocks in veterinary medicine," she said lightly, wishing he hadn't brought up this discussion so soon…or at all.

His eyes were forest-green, and she gazed into them, feeling aware of Nate Stanton in a way she'd never been aware of another man. Time seemed to stop.

Then he gave her another easy smile. "Spoken like a dedicated vet. Are you afraid you won't like Whisper Rock?" He seemed to be searching for answers to questions he'd formed since they'd last spoken.

"I'm sure I'll like Whisper Rock just fine. My grandmother lives in Phoenix, and it will be nice to be close to her again." Granna was getting older, the arthritis in her shoulder bothering her more. Fortunately, Brooke had taken the board exams and gotten licensed in Arizona a few years ago. She'd known she'd eventually return to the state, wanting time with Granna before it was too late.

Leaning against the counter now, Nate crossed his arms. "Do you get bored easily?"

She didn't know what she had said to give him the impression she might. "No, I don't get bored easily."

"You've practiced near Chicago, in Syracuse and now here."

Her heart sped up. "We covered that in our interview."

Nodding, he agreed, "Yes, we did. You said you enjoy seeing different parts of the country."

"That's right." She wanted to leave the explanation

right there. If he pushed her… "Are you having second thoughts about hiring me?"

He motioned to the counter with its triple stack of files. "No. I need assistance now. But I *would* like to know if you're going to stay for a day or a year. Or…if you might be running from the FBI." He said it with a trace of wry humor, but Brooke could see this was a man who wasn't satisfied with surface explanations.

"Dr. Stanton—"

"It's Nate."

She hesitated a moment. "All right. Nate. I'm not sure how long I'll stay. I told you that on the phone. More than a day, and I don't know about the year. But I can definitely assure you I'm not running from the FBI."

The handsome veterinarian raked his hand through his hair, and she could tell he was about to start in on another round of questions when the telephone rang.

Giving her a we'll-get-back-to-this-later look, he reached across the counter and picked up the phone from its console.

Nate listened to Everett McCoy while his attention was still focused on his new vet as she crouched to pet Frisco. There was something about her that drew his gaze to her again and again. There was also a scent surrounding her that reminded him of antique lace and verdant gardens. Everything about her was intriguing. Yet as Everett told Nate his problem, the rancher soon had Nate's full attention.

A few minutes later he switched off the phone and set it back on its console. "That was Everett McCoy. He has a ranch south of town. One of his cows is having a difficult time with labor. She's in trouble but won't let him get near her. I need to help out so he doesn't lose the calf.

Would you like to come along? Or do you need time to unwind after traveling?''

"I'm fine," she answered him enthusiastically. "I'd love to come."

"I just have to grab my jacket and bag," he said over his shoulder as he snatched both from his office and met up with her again in the reception area. "Do you want to ride along with me or drive out on your own?" he asked as he headed for the door, Frisco right behind him.

"I'll ride with you. My van's leaking some kind of fluid and I don't want to drive it too far."

As they stepped outside, Nate glanced at her van. It looked to be about eight years old. Maybe he could take a look under the hood when they got back. As he headed for his black SUV parked near the fenced-in yard, Brooke ran to keep up. He opened the back door and snapped his fingers for Frisco to jump inside. His canine best friend went most places with him. Why leave his pet fenced-in and alone when they could enjoy each other's company?

Brooke climbed in and fastened her seat belt. As Nate caught the scent surrounding her again, he found his eyes drawn to her profile.

After Frisco nosed Nate's neck, Nate jabbed his key into the ignition, and his dog settled on the back seat.

"How long have you had Frisco?" Brooke asked.

To take his mind off the way he was reacting to her, he shifted into reverse and thought back. "Seven years. I was working at a clinic on the West Coast when a passerby brought him in. He'd been hit by a car. I fixed him up and when no one claimed him, he became my best pal."

Brooke glanced over her shoulder and saw Frisco obediently sitting on the seat, peering curiously out the window. "He's well trained."

Making a U-turn, Nate drove to the exit of the parking lot and out onto the road. "I worked with him. He just has one bad habit. If he gets anywhere near a moving car, he chases it. I have to make sure I have the latch on the fence gate secured properly, because he's smart enough to undo it if I don't. The road in front of the clinic isn't that busy, but busy enough."

Snow fell faster as Nate drove to the McCoy ranch. Brooke was silent as she watched the sway of the windshield wipers and the scenery speeding by. He wondered what she was thinking.

A mile later they turned onto a stone-covered lane. Nate pointed to a fenced-in corral behind the barn where a cow was running wildly. "There she is."

After he parked the SUV by the big, red barn, he switched off the wipers. "I have everything we need in the back. The problem's going to be if she won't let us near her to examine her. We'll talk to Everett about giving her something to calm her down."

Nate assumed Brooke would follow him as he let Frisco out of the SUV and crossed to Everett McCoy, who'd come out of the barn. "What are the chances we can get her inside?" Nate asked the older man.

Rubbing his gray, beard-stubbled chin, Everett shook his head. "Not good. Hildy's as ornery as all get-out since she's been pregnant. We might have to chase her down and corner her, but I don't know what she'll do then."

As Nate glanced around the barn into the corral again, his heart almost stopped. "Brooke! Don't go in there," he yelled.

She waved that she'd heard him but paid him no heed as she closed the gate behind her and walked slowly toward the cow who had stopped for a moment by the far fence.

"What in the hell does she think she's going to do?" Everett asked. "Who is she, anyway?"

"She's coming into the practice with me. I just hired her."

"Ain't she got no brains?"

According to her résumé, Nate knew Brooke had handled ranch animals. But had she ever been in a corral before with a cow in labor who wanted no part of a veterinarian's help? "Brooke," he called again.

Either ignoring him or not hearing him, she kept approaching the animal.

Nate hurried toward the corral, really worried now, Everett close at his heels. But as he opened the gate and went inside, he suddenly stopped. Brooke had her hand on the cow's neck. She was talking to her in soothing tones. Nate noticed the satchel draped over her shoulder. Had she given the animal something?

As he and Everett stared in amazement, the cow folded onto the ground and Brooke lowered herself beside her. A moment later the pretty vet took off her coat, reached inside her satchel and pulled out a pair of latex gloves. She didn't seem to notice that snow was collecting on her hair.

"Brooke, this isn't safe," Nate warned in a low voice that he hoped wouldn't startle the cow. "She could kick out at you at any minute."

But Brooke was already examining the cow, one hand and arm inside, her other hand on the animal's belly. "Stay by her head, Nate. Talk to her. Soothe her. Her baby's caught. I almost have him…"

Nate knelt beside the cow and put his large hand on her head, marveling at her quietness under Brooke's handling.

The cow's legs started moving and Brooke said, "It's okay, girl. Just a little longer... There!"

During the next few minutes Nate watched as Brooke soothed and encouraged Hildy. They waited and watched as the cow finally pushed her baby into the world. The calf's forelegs protruded first, and then there it was in all its newborn glory.

Everett came over to them. "Well, by golly. I never thought I'd see Hildy this gentled."

Already recovering, Hildy was taking over her duties as a mama by licking and warming her calf.

"How in blue-blazes did you do that?" Everett asked Brooke.

Brooke was watching mother and calf with an expression on her face that Nate would like to capture for a lifetime. He knew the miracle of birth had touched her as it always touched him. For some insane reason, he wanted to capture Brooke Pennington's hand in his, tell her he understood....

She whisked off her gloves and gave the old rancher a small shrug. "It was just time she let someone help her."

Nate and Everett exchanged a look. Then the rancher just shrugged and grinned. "I don't care how you did it. It looks like I got a healthy calf and Hildy's in good shape. That's all that matters."

Suddenly Nate didn't know if that *was* all that mattered. He wasn't as gullible as Everett, and he wanted to know exactly how Brooke had quieted the animal.

A half hour later, mother and calf were ensconced in a stall in the barn. Hildy had let Everett lead her inside, while Nate had carried her baby and Brooke had washed up.

After Nate and Brooke said goodbye to the rancher, Nate had one thing on his mind—finding out what Brooke had done to that cow. Frisco happily perched on the back seat of the SUV as Brooke climbed in. She hadn't said much while Everett had gotten Hildy and her newborn settled in the barn.

Nate switched on the ignition, then the windshield wipers. As they brushed away accumulated snow, he asked, "What did you give her?"

A few seconds passed before Brooke replied, "I didn't give her anything."

Stealing a look at his new associate, he frowned. "You can't tell me she just let you walk up to her and help her down to the ground."

Brooke nodded. "She did. Maybe she just needed a woman's touch."

Nate grunted and cast another sideways glance at her. "You expect me to believe that?"

"As I told you during the interview, I don't use drugs if I don't have to. I prefer more natural remedies."

Natural. That was definitely the word that applied to Brooke. But he still didn't quite believe she had sweet-talked that animal to the ground. This woman was a puzzle, and in spite of himself Nate wanted to figure her out.

Doing her best to stay calm, Brooke stared straight ahead as Nate drove, watching the patterns the swirls of snow made as they fell onto the windshield. She could feel Nate glancing at her every now and then. Each time he did, there was a quickening inside of her. It had begun the very moment she'd looked into his deep-green eyes. Yet she knew she shouldn't be attracted to him. He was a no-nonsense kind of man with more questions than she wanted to answer.

She wondered why he looked familiar. There was something about the set of his defined jaw, his rugged profile, his thick, black hair. She didn't know much about him—just that he'd opened his practice in Whisper Rock three years ago. He'd lived above the veterinary clinic until fall when he'd helped the contractor with the construction of his house. She suddenly wondered if he intended to share it with someone other than Frisco.

Why was she even wondering? Even if she wanted to stay here, it was only a matter of time until she'd have to move on.

Ten minutes later Nate parked in front of the clinic. Brooke was about to exit the car when he clasped her arm. Although the fabric of her coat was between his hand and her skin, it seemed as if she could feel his touch through the wool. Her whole body tingled. When she looked up into his eyes, she knew what she'd felt for Tim three long years ago hadn't had the element of primal awareness that she now felt with Nate.

"I don't know what you did with Hildy, but thanks for saving her calf," Nate said with sincerity.

"If I'm working for you, that's just part of my job."

"You're working for me," he replied.

With the snow enveloping everything outside, heat seemed to build in the car. Nate cleared his throat. "Would you like to see the apartment now?"

"That would be good," she murmured, feeling breathless, knowing the sensation wasn't from the altitude.

Nate released her arm and nodded. "Let's go have a look."

As soon as Brooke stepped into the studio apartment, she liked it. It had double windows on two walls, and even though it was a cloudy day she could tell there would be lots of light. The walls were painted a pleasant mint-green and the space felt welcoming to her. There was a stove, a microwave and a small refrigerator, a dinette table with a Formica top and four chrome and red vinyl chairs.

The double bed had a dark pine bookcase headboard and a nightstand beside it. The sleeping area was separated from the rest of the space by a tan leather sofa.

"You can fix it up however you'd like," Nate said. "I never bothered with curtains, just blinds. But I'll put up fixtures if that's what you want."

"I don't need curtains. I like the additional light without them. You didn't need the bed?"

"That bed's just a double because it's all I could get in here. I bought a king-size suite for the house. My furniture and appliances are supposed to be delivered on Monday."

The bed was sheetless and there were no personal belongings anywhere. "Have you already moved?"

"Yep. I had finish work to do so I've been sleeping on an air mattress over there. I have a microwave and that's all I need until the rest arrives."

Brooke couldn't keep her gaze from passing over Nate's long body. He had to be at least six-two. It was too easy to envision him in the new king-size bed he'd bought. "You don't need the sofa, either?"

"It's pretty lumpy. I bought it in a second-hand store when I moved in."

"Living on a budget?" she asked with a smile.

"I didn't know how long it would take to build up the practice, but I also knew I wanted my own house someday. I guess you could say I've been frugal. A partner buying into the practice would give me capital to expand or to pay off some of my mortgage," he added casually, trying to draw her into that discussion once more.

Before he could delve deeper into the partnership issue, she took them back to the reason for being here. "I'd like living up here. I'll drive to the motel, pick up my suitcases and check out."

Nate glanced at his watch. "I'm meeting the electrician over at the house in a little while. If you need help moving in when you get back, just give a yell."

She was used to taking care of herself, and she certainly didn't want to depend on Nate when she was so attracted to him. "I'll be fine. What time do your appointments start in the morning?"

"Nine o'clock. I have patients scheduled for every fifteen minutes until noon, and I'm sure there will be some walk-ins. There always are. I'll be able to put you to work right away. Maybe I'll actually get a lunch hour for a change."

The warm humor in Nate's eyes was like a soothing balm to Brooke, and his wry grin made her belly flip-flop. If she was going to work with this man, she had to rein in the attraction she felt toward him. She couldn't get involved. Not just because she might only be here for a few months, but because she didn't trust easily anymore. Tim's rejection had hurt her deeply. He hadn't merely rejected her love but the core of who she was. Actually, the sole human she trusted was Granna. It would be so good to see her again.

Brooke took a few steps away from Nate toward the door. "Thanks for offering me the apartment. After I move in, I'd like to look at your files and become better acquainted with your practice."

Taking a key ring from his pocket, Nate slipped off two of the keys. Crossing to her, he held them out. "The rounded one is for the apartment. The square one is for the clinic."

Carefully she took the keys without touching his hand. It was better if she kept her distance. It was better if they became polite colleagues instead of close friends. She had to live her life that way. She had no choice.

After she thanked him again, she left the apartment, but she could feel his gaze on her back as she went down the stairs. She didn't turn around.

Nate had put Frisco in his yard before showing her the apartment. The dog ran to the fence and barked as she made a U-turn in her van and left the clinic's parking lot.

On her drive to the motel, Brooke was still thinking about the way a thatch of Nate's hair fell over his forehead and wondering why he looked so familiar whenever it happened.

The snow had slowed, but as she watched the road, smoke began seeping from under her van's hood. At first she thought it was vapor from heat meeting cold, but then the engine coughed and sputtered and continued sputtering. By the time she turned into the motel parking lot, a cloud was puffing from the van. Although she was dismayed, she was grateful she had reached Whisper Rock safely. This could have happened anywhere on her trek from Syracuse to here.

At the motel, she went inside her room and called the emergency service number for her auto club. She was directed to a service station in Flagstaff, and by the time she phoned there and arranged for towing, another fifteen minutes had passed. She thought about renting a car, but decided to wait until a mechanic figured out what was wrong and how long her car would be out of commission. That left only one thing to do. Call Nate.

Usually she didn't call anyone for help. Because Brooke's parents had never been married, because they'd abandoned her and left her with her paternal grandmother while they'd gallivanted the globe on a whim and little cash, Brooke had always felt as if she couldn't depend on anyone but herself...and Granna. She had lived with fierce independence for so long that when Tim Peabody had come along, she'd been afraid to take a chance on becoming involved. She'd been afraid to believe that Tim could accept who she really was. She'd been right to be afraid. When he'd found out her means of healing some of her furry patients were unorthodox—

Only Granna accepted who she was, and Brooke suspected that's the way it always would be. That's why she depended only on herself. That's why she didn't usually call anyone for help. Now, however, she had no choice.

Taking Nate's business card from her wallet, she dialed the number on it. When the answering machine picked up, she ended the connection and dialed the second number listed.

Nate answered on the first ring. "Veterinary clinic."

She smiled because his answer had been so automatic. His profession was obviously the focus of his life. "Hi, Nate. It's Brooke. My van gave out on the way here to the motel and I'm waiting for the tow truck. I'll be back as soon as they check it out and I've rented a car."

"Do you really want to do that?"

Smiling again, she remembered Nate was frugal. "I really don't have a choice."

"Sure, you do. I'll look at the van before the truck picks it up and give you an idea of what's going on. I could always give you a lift into Flagstaff when you need it. If you're living above the clinic, you won't need your car to get to work," he added with some amusement.

If she postponed her trip to Granna's until after the car was fixed, all she'd need were a few groceries and she'd be set. "Are you sure you don't mind? This is above and beyond the call of an employer."

Again there was a pause. "I don't mind, Brooke. One thing you learn quickly about Whisper Rock is the helpfulness of its residents. People actually smile at you here…and wave. They'd also pick you up if they saw you stranded on the highway. That's why I live here."

"You make it sound ideal."

"It is…for *me*. Sit tight. I'll be there in five minutes." He hung up before she could even say thank you.

When Nate arrived at the parking lot of the motel and saw Brooke standing by her van waiting for him, he felt a little bit like a white knight. It had been a while since he'd rescued a damsel in distress. Looking at Brooke, feeling the bite of desire her appearance had triggered when she'd arrived, he was glad it was her he was rescuing.

As soon as he approached her, she said, "Thanks for doing this." He saw she really did appreciate it. Didn't she expect people she knew to help her?

"I didn't do anything yet." He unlatched the hood of her car and examined the engine. It only took him a few minutes to determine the problem. "You need a new head gasket. You're going to have a whopping bill with this one."

"Cars," she said with a frown. "Sometimes I think a horse would be more economical."

He shut the hood and saw that she knew full well how much the upkeep of a horse would be. "I don't know," he teased. "You'd get wet on a rainy day."

She laughed. "I guess I would. But I think the ride would be a lot more enjoyable."

What he already liked about Brooke was her flexibility. Another woman in her shoes might have gotten frazzled by an unexpected vet call before she even had her office set up. Another woman might have gotten totally frazzled by what had just happened with the van. But Brooke seemed to be rolling with the punches. Had moving from place to place made her that way? He still wanted to know why she didn't seem inclined to put down roots. Roots were all-important to him now—roots and anonymity. Before he'd moved to Whisper Rock from L.A., he'd had enough of being in the spotlight for a lifetime. His famous father and the course his own life had almost taken now led him to seek peace and quiet rather than excitement.

The tow truck arrived soon after Nate checked the van. They unloaded it and packed her things in the back of his SUV. He was curious about a small cedar chest, which Brooke seemed to take extra care with. It was heavy for its size, but that weight came from its solid mahogany wood as well as the contents.

When they arrived back at the clinic, he suggested, "Anything you don't want cluttering up your apartment I can store in my garage."

She looked over her shoulder at the cedar chest and then the steep flight of stairs leading up to the apartment over the clinic. "The chest can go in the garage. Everything else I'll take up. But you don't have to help. I can manage. I know you probably have things to do. Especially since it's your day off."

"Hopefully, hiring you will give me more free time, so don't worry about my day off. Come on. With two of us lugging, we'll have it all up there in fifteen minutes."

He was right. Although the stairs had given them a workout, most of the boxes were light. Her two suitcases and garment bag had been easy to handle.

Hanging the garment bag in the closet near the bed, Nate said, "There are many women who would need a few more suitcases to carry all their clothing. Or are you having the rest of your things sent?"

"This is it."

Brooke propped a pair of cross-country skis in a corner and took off her coat. Her soft aqua sweater molded to her breasts. It had short sleeves and hugged her slender waist. Nate found himself moving toward her, studying the curve of her dark brown brows, the delicate straightness of her nose, her pretty oval face framed by hair that looked as soft as silk.

To distract himself from the desire that gripped him, he tried to put practical concerns in its place. "You're going to need groceries. One of my day-off errands is to stock up. If you want to unpack, I still have work to do at the house. We can go later."

The space between them seemed to vibrate with awareness...with electricity...with man-woman tension. Did she feel the hum between them, too? When her lips parted slightly, he found himself leaning a bit closer. He finally figured out what the wonderful scent was that surrounded her—she smelled like lavender.

Just as he thought about bending his head to kiss her, he heard a car turning into the parking lot, the crunch of gravel, a revved-up engine. Maybe it was an emergency.

Whatever it was, he straightened, glad something had jolted him out of the haze that had overtaken him. He hadn't been seriously involved with a woman since his fiancée broke off their engagement three and a half years ago. He shouldn't think of getting involved now... especially not with a woman who was here today and might be gone tomorrow.

Clearing his throat, he stepped away from Brooke. "I'd better see who just drove in." He headed for the apartment door.

"Let me know if you need me," she said lightly, obviously expecting a patient, too.

He nodded. But he knew he wouldn't let himself need Brooke Pennington in any way that mattered.

Chapter Two

On Friday morning Brooke listened to the mechanic on the phone and frowned.

"We can't finish your van until Tuesday," he informed her. "We're backed up today and closed over the weekend."

A few moments later she hung up, thinking about her plans. If she wanted to see Granna this weekend, she'd have to rent a car to drive to Phoenix. So be it. She suddenly needed to feel her grandmother's hug. She needed to feel her only true connection in this world.

Yesterday she'd felt a connection to Nate—an extraordinary connection. She'd seen the desire in his eyes and felt her heart thunder as she'd waited for his kiss. Then he'd backed away, and she'd realized getting involved would have been sheer stupidity—an open invitation to more heartache. When she'd accompanied him to the grocery store last evening, they'd acted like strangers who were going to work together. It was best if she kept to herself. It was best if she stopped this attraction to Nate Stanton before it even got started.

Resolved about that now, she just wanted to hear her grandmother's voice. After she checked her watch, she dialed the number. Although it was only 8:00 a.m., she knew her grandmother would be in the kitchen after feeding the horses. Granna was seventy-two now. But the sparkle in her brown eyes spoke of an inner fire that would always burn brightly. Brooke missed Granna so. She hadn't seen her in six long months.

Anna Pennington picked up on the second ring. "Good morning," she greeted whoever might be calling.

Brooke couldn't remember when she had started calling her grandmother "Granna." Maybe Anna Pennington herself had encouraged it, since she was somewhere in between a grandmother and a mother to Brooke. It had just seemed to always fit.

"Granna, it's Brooke."

"Oh, Brooke, honey! I'm so glad you called. Where are you?"

"I'm in Whisper Rock, only three hours from you. My van needs some work done, but I can't wait to see you. I think I'll rent a car and drive down on Sunday. Is that all right?"

There were a few moments of silence, and Brooke's heart started pounding faster. Something was wrong. "Granna?"

"Don't be alarmed, Brooke. I'm just trying to figure out how to say what I have to say to you."

"What? Is something wrong? Are you sick?"

"No. No, not me."

"Not you?"

Brooke almost felt her grandmother take a long, calming breath. "This is how it is, honey. Your father's here."

It had been four years since Brooke had seen her dad. He was living outside of Paris now, and the last time she'd spoken with him he'd had no intention of coming back to the United States anytime soon.

"Does he have Tessa with him?" she asked her grandmother. Tessa was the half sister she'd never met, the half sister who would be a little over three now.

"Yes. Tessa's here, too."

"Why did he come?" Cal Pennington had left the ranch outside of Phoenix a few weeks after he'd graduated from high school. Her grandmother had always told Brooke he had wanderlust.

"Cal has to have a surgery...carotid artery surgery."

Brooke swallowed hard. "When?"

"Next week. He's been here over a week, seeing doctors, having tests. His doctor insists his condition is a ticking bomb if he doesn't have the operation."

"Was he having symptoms?" Brooke knew her father's condition was more serious if he was.

"Headaches. Some dizziness. Weakness in his left arm."

"Why did he come to Phoenix?"

"So I can help him."

Her grandmother's answer summed up everything about her father's selfishness.

"Brooke?"

"Yes. I'm here."

"Are you still coming on Sunday? I know Cal wants to see you."

Brooke wished that was true. After she was born, neither of her parents had wanted her. That's why they'd left her with Granna. When her mother died a year later, her father hadn't claimed her. Apparently he'd decided perfunctory visits a couple of times a year were adequate. "Has he told you he wants to see me?"

"Yes, he has."

"He didn't want to see me after Helena died." Her father had finally married at fifty. His wife had died from breast cancer last year, and Brooke had tried to connect with him again, offering to fly to France. But Cal Pennington had insisted she not disrupt her life, and she'd gotten the message that he wanted to grieve alone. She'd felt like that unwanted child again—the child he'd left behind.

"I don't know what was going on in his head then, any more than I ever have. But I do know he's facing his mortality now," Granna offered.

"And he wants to have a heart-to-heart with me?"

"Possibly. I don't know, Brooke. You have to do what's best for you."

So many thoughts swirled in Brooke's mind. Granna had always taught her to follow her own path. Uppermost was the knowledge she'd never met her half sister. She felt countless emotions where Tessa was concerned. Apparently, her father had embraced this child he'd had so late in his life instead of abandoning her as he had Brooke.

Maybe it was time Brooke confronted all of it head-on. "I'll be there on Sunday."

"Can you stay overnight?"

"No. Not with just starting my job here. Today's my first day and I don't want to take time off so soon."

"No, I suppose you don't. I can't wait to see you, honey. Drive carefully on your way down."

"I will. I'll see you Sunday."

When Brooke returned the handset to its cradle, she thought about all the years in which she'd wondered if her father loved her. She thought about the fact that her parents had been unmarried and the reality that her mother had wanted to have an abortion. Cal Pennington had asked his mother to take Brooke instead. She'd heard the explanation often. He'd been young, wild, restless and in love with a woman who didn't want children. Yet he hadn't wanted Gail to abort their child, either. Apparently Granna's views on the sacredness of life had been handed down to her son. Still after Brooke's mother died, he'd insisted he didn't know how to raise a child and Brooke was better off with Granna.

Brooke suspected she *had* been better off with Granna. But she still didn't know if her father had ever loved her. Maybe Sunday would bring her answers.

When Brooke descended the stairs a short while later, she stepped up onto the clinic's porch. After she pushed open the door, she entered, trying to put everything her grandmother had told her out of her mind. She saw Nate first. He was standing behind the receptionist's counter, making notations on charts. The papers in his hand looked like results from lab work. He was wearing blue jeans and a navy, long-sleeved Henley shirt.

"Good morning." When he looked up, the sparks of desire in his eyes belied his polite tone. He was also giving her the same polite smile he'd used several times last night while they were grocery shopping.

He motioned to the middle-aged, auburn-haired woman sitting at the desk. "Brooke, this is Ellie Yardwick. She's my all-round right hand for taking care of the billing and the paperwork and whatever else needs to be done. Ellie, meet Brooke Pennington, our new vet on staff."

After giving Brooke an assessing once-over, Ellie extended her hand. "It's good to have you here, Dr. Pennington. Maybe now Nate will even have time for lunch. And…maybe a life."

Brooke liked the older woman, who appeared to be in her fifties. "Please call me Brooke. I'm eager to get started. Can you show me the lineup for this morning?"

Ellie handed her a sheet of paper. "The patients circled in red will be yours today. Mostly routine stuff—rabies shots, thyroid checks. Mr. Carlson's dog, Bones, has a sore paw."

As Brooke took the list from Ellie, along with the files that had been stacked under it, she said, "I'll take these to my office and go over them."

"If you have questions about anything, just give a holler. Nate's writing is sometimes hard to read," the receptionist warned her.

Frisco, who had been sitting next to Ellie's chair, came over to Brooke then, sniffed her hand and brushed his tail against her leg.

"Hi, there, fella. Good morning to you, too." She looked up at Nate. "Does he stay in here with you?"

"Usually he sits out here with Ellie. He likes the comings and goings. He's a combination protector and good-luck charm."

Rising to her feet, she gave the dog a pat on the head. Switching the charts into the crook of her arm, she said to Ellie, "Let me know when my first patient arrives." Then she headed for her office. Nate would have gone into his office next door, but she lightly touched his arm. "Nate?"

His eyes met hers, and she saw distance there. Good. That was best for both of them. "Have you used any of the rental car companies in Flagstaff? I wondered who you'd recommend."

"I told you I'd be glad to take you anywhere you'd like to go."

"I'm sure you didn't have a three-hour drive to Phoenix

in mind. I have to see my grandmother on Sunday. I really can't put it off.''

"When will your car be finished?"

"Tuesday morning. But I must get down there this weekend.''

"Problems?"

"I'm not exactly sure. I..." She stopped, not used to confiding in anyone about her life.

Apparently Nate could see that something was troubling her. "Is something wrong with your grandmother?"

"No. It's...complicated.''

"Family matters usually are," he said wryly, as if he knew. After studying her for a few moments, he decided, "It seems silly to rent a car for a day. They'll charge you an arm and a leg. I have a friend who lives in Phoenix, and I haven't seen him for a few months. When I spoke to Ramón last week, he said he was free this weekend. Why don't I run you down, spend the day with him and then bring you home?''

"You're being much too kind.''

His eyes were gentle now as he asked, "Aren't you used to kindness?"

People were kind until they were faced with something they didn't understand. Then, even friends became strangers and kindness was a thing of the past. "I guess I'm just not used to someone going out of his way to help me.''

Nate shrugged. "I'm not really helping you. I planned to see Ramón anyway.''

"What about the clinic? Aren't you on call?"

"I have an arrangement with a vet in Flagstaff. We cover for each other. I'll call him and see if Sunday's okay.''

"I really appreciate everything you're doing to help me settle in."

"I have an ulterior motive. I want you to stay."

At least he was honest. Still, she felt she needed to do something in return. "To show my appreciation, let me cook supper for you tomorrow night. You still don't have appliances, right?"

"Right. But you don't need to do that."

"If tomorrow night isn't good and you have plans...we can do it another time."

He seemed to debate with himself for a few moments. Then he shook his head. "No, I don't have plans. Tomorrow night will be fine. What time?"

"Around seven?"

"Seven's good. What can I bring?"

Already planning the menu, she smiled. "An open mind." She was a vegetarian and she'd introduce him to something a little different.

"Uh-oh. Is this going to be an adventure?"

"Possibly. But nothing too wild, I promise."

The bell over the door in the waiting room sounded, and the barking of two boxers broke the morning silence.

"We're off and running," Nate said with a grin. "If you have any problems or questions, don't hesitate to ask."

"I won't," she assured him, and then went into her office to prepare herself for the first day of her position in Whisper Rock...wondering how long she'd be here...wondering why she found the green of Nate's eyes so fascinating...wondering why the trip to Phoenix on Sunday now didn't seem quite so daunting.

As Brooke put the vegetarian fare in front of Nate Saturday evening, he took a whiff of all of it and felt his stomach rumble. To his surprise, it all smelled good.

She pointed to each dish on the table. "That's a red chili, pasta, cheese and bean casserole. The cabbage salad has a sweet-and-sour dressing, and the bread is made with cornmeal. Watch out for the broccoli soup. It's a bit peppery."

When she set the soup bowl in front of him, the smell wafted up and made his mouth water. "You went to a lot of trouble." They'd both worked in the clinic for the morning, but then Nate had gone to his house to hammer trim into place, and obviously Brooke had planned their meal.

"I enjoy cooking. It's much more fun doing it for two."

Nate took a piece of cornbread and slathered it with butter, determined to satisfy one appetite if not another. "Have you cooked for two often?" He was curious about her past and what had brought her here.

Seated across from him, she met his gaze. "What would you like to know?"

He gave her a wry grimace. "I'm not too subtle, am I? I just wondered if you'd ever been married." It was possible she was running from an ex-husband or an ex-something.

"No, I've never been married. I was seriously involved a few years ago, but it didn't work out. How about you?"

Fair was fair, he supposed. "I was involved a few years ago. Engaged, actually. But it didn't work out, either."

As the room seemed to vibrate with silence, Nate realized there were volumes that neither of them were saying. It was obvious that Brooke didn't confide easily. He didn't, either. He thought about the circus he'd escaped from—his actor father, his own brief fling in the limelight, the family scandal that had broken apart his engagement.

A few minutes later, finished with the soup, he set the dish aside and scooped out a helping of the casserole. "When did you become a vegetarian?"

"When I was a teenager."

His fork stopped in midair. "You became health conscious that early?"

She served herself a portion of the casserole. "It depends on what you mean by health conscious. I didn't have a condition I had to watch or anything like that. I just found I had more…energy and felt better on a vegetarian diet. Granna helped me explore recipes to make meals interesting."

"That's a unique name."

"She's my grandmother and her name is Anna."

"You spent a lot of time with her when you were a child?"

"She raised me."

There was something in that quiet, simple statement that made it not so simple at all. "You lost your parents?"

Brooke slid the bowl of slaw from the side of the table and offered Nate some. He nodded. "Everything's very good."

"Thank you."

They were both aware that she hadn't answered his question. "You don't want to talk about your family?"

"I have mixed feelings about the way I grew up. I love Granna, and she took wonderful care of me. I did lose my parents, but not exactly the way you mean. My parents left me with Granna right after I was born." She took a piece of bread from the basket. "I'm going to Phoenix tomorrow because my dad has to have carotid artery surgery, and I feel as if I should see him before he does. I've never met my half sister, and she's at the ranch, too.''

After a pause she asked, ''How about you? Where do you come from originally?''

Digesting what she'd said, he thought about the half brother *he'd* never met. With the divorce rate and families splitting, step-brothers and sisters, half brothers and sisters were commonplace now. Seeing Brooke watching him expectantly, he offered some of his history. ''I was born in Chicago. But my parents and I moved around a lot when I was a kid. I spent most of my life in California.''

Brooke went to the counter and switched on the coffeemaker. After she took her seat again, she asked, ''Did you have your own clinic there?''

''I was in a practice with two other vets. The friend I'm going to see tomorrow in Phoenix was my mentor in college—one of my professors. He retired the year after I graduated, and that summer I came out here to visit him. On my way to Phoenix I drove through Whisper Rock. When I decided my life needed a change, I moved here.''

The way Brooke was studying him told him she knew that there was way more behind his words than the simple explanation he'd given. But she didn't question him further and he knew she wanted the same courtesy. The thing was, he found himself wanting to delve much deeper with Brooke. He didn't know what it was about her. She was beautiful, intelligent, and after the way she'd handled the animals today, he knew she was compassionate and caring. She was a mystery he wanted to solve. Yet an inner alarm warned him to be cautious.

They moved to the sofa for coffee and a lemon dessert that melted in Nate's mouth. They talked about snowmobiling and skiing in the area, the animals they'd seen and the owners who'd brought them in. He filled her in on the Whisper Rock community, telling her about the daily newspaper, the new mall to be built in the spring and the landmark that gave the town its name.

After she placed her dish on the coffee table, she asked, "So there really is a Whisper Rock?"

"Sure is. On the north side of town on a bluff overlooking the valley. If you sit at the base of the rock and listen very carefully, it will whisper to you."

"Has it ever whispered to you?"

She was sitting close, her shoulder grazing his. She was close enough for him to smell her lavender scent…close enough for him to see the pure creaminess of her skin…close enough for him to feel desire.

Leaning forward, he picked up his coffee and took a swallow. Then he explained, "The first time I came to Arizona and stayed here, I think it was Whisper Rock that made me want to learn more about the place. So in its way I guess it *did* whisper to me."

He thought of sitting at the base of that rock with her, watching the sunset, feeling the breeze. He thought about his ex-fiancée, Linda, the concerts and plays they'd attended, the upscale restaurants. He thought about her little girl, Kristi, and how giving up the idea of being a father had been almost as difficult to deal with as their broken engagement.

It was time to go, time to put this evening with Brooke into perspective. "I'd better be going if we're going to leave around eight tomorrow morning. I have to check on our boarders and give them some kibble before I turn in."

If she was disappointed that he wasn't staying, she didn't show it. "Need help?"

"Pouring kibble for two Pekingese? I don't think so. By the way, their owner is picking them up in the morning. Ellie said she'll come in and handle it." Standing, he said, "I could help you clean up the kitchen."

"No need for that. There isn't that much."

"Everything was great."

"I'm glad you liked it."

He felt both relieved and disappointed when he lifted his jacket from the back of the sofa. After he shrugged into it, she walked him to the door. To his surprise she stepped outside with him. She looked up at the sky as if she were counting the stars.

He motioned to the thousand twinkles of light. "I've never seen stars like this anywhere else."

"The sky *is* beautiful. I can see why you chose to live here."

He couldn't help clasping her shoulder and nudging her around. "You could choose it, too."

There was a sadness in her eyes that he wanted to take away...a hope he wanted to build on. Logically he knew it was too soon for that. Her white sweater was soft under his fingers, and he could feel the heat of her skin under it, the narrow strap of her bra. His nerve endings were jumping, and the longer they stood under the dark sky, the more aroused he became. Sensing the deep passion in her, decorum and logic seemed not to matter. Slipping his hand under her hair, he cupped the back of her head.

She went perfectly still, searching his face. When he bent his head, she was still searching. But then her eyelids fluttered shut and he took her mouth. The press of his lips on hers wasn't nearly enough. His tongue breached her lips and waited for a response. She came alive in his arms, all heat and passion and answering desire. The intensity of the kiss rocked him, and he ended it, stunned because simple had turned into complicated in less than a heartbeat.

The kiss had been a mistake. He needed more than chemistry...more than a woman who was here today and gone tomorrow. He was sorry now he'd accepted her invitation to dinner.

"Nate..." she began.

"It's all right, Brooke. I shouldn't have done that. I'll see you in the morning."

Sadness was back in her eyes again. But he couldn't be concerned about that. Everyone had secrets. It was better if he didn't know Brooke's and she didn't know his.

When Nate pulled up in front of Granna's on Sunday, the ranch house looked to Brooke as it always did, with its shell-pink stucco and the clay-tiled roof. Oleander grew beside the front door attesting to the fact that the temperature in Phoenix was at least twenty degrees warmer than in Flagstaff. During the drive, Brooke had slipped off her jacket. She thought about the Miles Davis jazz that had filled the car instead of conversation. After that kiss last night, she didn't know what to say or how to act with Nate. Now, upon their arrival, she didn't know whether to invite him in or not.

That decision was taken out of her hands as her grandmother came out of the house, grinning from ear to ear. Granna's long, straight hair, more gray now than brown, was held at her nape with a wooden barrette. Her navy-and-rust cotton skirt flowed to her ankles, just hitting the top of her short, deerskin boots.

Dashing from Nate's car without thinking twice about it, Brooke had her arms around her grandmother.

Granna hugged her as she always had, with the confidence and strength of a woman who knew her place in the world. She kissed Brooke's cheek and then leaned away. "It's been too long."

At the end of last summer when she'd taken her two-week vacation, Brooke had flown out to see her grandmother. Since then they'd spoken on the phone and written each other letters. Nevertheless, nothing could replace an actual hug.

Brooke saw her grandmother gazing speculatively at Nate's SUV. "Nate drove and saved me the expense of renting a car," she explained.

Brooke felt pressure against her thigh, and she glanced down to see Frisco looking up at her expectantly, as if he wanted to be introduced.

Granna laughed. "Is this a new friend?"

When Nate came up beside Brooke, Granna gave him a more appraising perusal than she'd given the dog. "You must be Nate Stanton." She extended her hand. "I'm Anna Pennington."

Nate shook her hand. "It's good to meet you. I thought I'd let Frisco stretch his legs and do whatever he needs to do before we drive out to Scottsdale to visit with a friend."

"Give him the run of the place, if you'd like. There are no other dogs here right now. Since Brooke left, we don't have a menagerie anymore."

"Did she rescue animals?" Nate asked with a conspiratorial smile.

"More than you could count. Always found a home for them, too, or returned them to the wild. My guess is you were like that, too, if you became a vet."

"Actually, I wasn't. Frisco was my first rescue. He and I got along so well, I couldn't bear to give him up to somebody else."

"Would you like to come in for a cup of coffee?" Granna asked. "I have some sweet rolls, too—"

The front screen door on the house banged shut. Brooke

turned and inhaled sharply. A little girl with chin-length, curly, dark-brown hair and huge brown eyes came running toward them.

As emotion washed over her, Brooke stood perfectly still. This was her sister.

Half sister, a small voice corrected her.

Tessa stood close to Granna's leg, almost behind her skirt, and peeked up.

Granna's voice was light. "Honey, this is Brooke. Say hello."

Dressed in denim overalls and a bright-red blouse and sweater, Tessa Pennington stepped in front of Granna. Her wide-eyed gaze met Brooke's. "Daddy says I'm gonna stay wif you. He has to go to the…hos-pi-tal." She drew out the word as if it was a new one she didn't quite understand. Dropping her gaze shyly, Tessa pointed to Frisco. "I like doggies."

Tessa thought she was going to stay with her? Brooke took a deep breath, stayed calm and focused on Tessa's comment. "Frisco belongs to Nate."

Poking two fingers into her mouth, Tessa asked around them, "C'n I pet him?" Her voice was sweetly high and uncertain.

This little girl was adorable, and Brooke was overcome with the urge to take Tessa into her arms and give her a mighty hug. Part of her wanted to make friends and form bonds so the child would always be a part of her life. But another part of her warned her to be careful. She had no idea what her father really wanted, what he was going to do or where he would go next.

Nate crouched down and smiled at Tessa. "He'd like for you to pet him. He also likes to be scratched between his ears."

Tessa was happily petting Frisco when the front screen

door banged again and Cal Pennington stepped outside. Brooke felt such a multitude of emotions she thought she'd burst. She was filled with the heartache of never feeling loved by him, along with the resentment of feeling abandoned, riding piggy-back on the hope that maybe now everything between them could change.

After Tessa glanced over her shoulder, she ran to her father, throwing her arms around his legs. Bending, he scooped up his little girl with his right arm while his left hung by his side. Brooke felt unsettled and raw and uncertain about what she was doing here.

Suddenly Nate gave her arm a squeeze. "You have the number I gave you so you can call when you're ready to leave?"

Unexpectedly she didn't want Nate to go, but that was ridiculous. "Yes, I have it."

Nate nodded. "I'll see you in a few hours." Then he gave her arm another squeeze as if in reassurance, and she realized what a perceptive man he was.

As Nate drove away, Brooke met her father's eyes, knowing Cal Pennington was going to disrupt her life and then leave again—as he had so many times before.

Chapter Three

After Granna corralled Tessa and took her into the house, Brooke faced her father. "It's been a long time." She didn't know exactly what to say to him or how to act. There had always been this awkwardness between them.

Cal didn't move, just studied her as if he was seeing her for the first time. "Tessa looks almost exactly like you did at her age."

Her heart leaped that he'd made the connection. "You remember?"

"I remember."

There was that awkward silence between them again, and Brooke moved to fill it. "Granna said you're ill."

"Yep. My carotid artery is clogged. The doc has to clean it out. That's why I came back here."

He was pale and much thinner than she remembered. "There aren't specialists in Paris?"

"Granna isn't in Paris, and neither are you. When she

told me you were taking a job in Arizona, I knew this is where I had to come.''

"I don't understand.''

"If something happens to me, I want Tessa to be here with you and Granna.''

For a multitude of reasons, his words shocked Brooke. "Nothing's going to happen to you.''

He shrugged. "I hope not. But if for some reason the surgery isn't successful— The thing is, Brooke, you and Granna are Tessa's only family. Helena was an only child and her parents died years ago.''

Brooke hadn't known much about her father's late wife, and she hadn't asked questions. "Family never seemed important to you before.'' The hurt from feeling abandoned all those years tinged her words.

After he frowned, he admitted, "I understand why you'd think that. But with Helena and Tessa, I learned things I never knew before. I'm realizing what I missed by letting Granna raise you, even though I felt I had no choice.''

"Because my mother didn't want me?''

"Gail couldn't take care of herself, let alone a child. And I wasn't much better. We were nineteen, Brooke.''

Brooke had never before spoken about any of this to her father, although she'd discussed it with Granna. She'd always felt removed from him...an afterthought. "I never felt I *had* a father. I never felt—'' She stopped, embarrassed by the emotion that choked her.

Shifting, he jabbed one hand into the pocket of his jeans. "Granna did right by you. That's what matters. And I know both of you will do right by Tessa if I don't make it. Your Granna's getting older...slowing down.'' He looked up at the sky, then toed the stones at his feet with his boot. "I want to name you as legal guardian of Tessa before I have surgery. I'm going to see a lawyer about it tomorrow."

When Nate checked his watch it was almost three. He and Ramón Martinez had gone out for lunch and then come back to Ramón's condo and watched basketball for a while. Now they'd taken beers out onto the terrace with Frisco following behind.

Ramón was in his late sixties, but still a dashing man with his steel-gray hair and thick mustache. "You haven't said much about your family." His attitude was casual as he took a swig from the long-necked bottle.

Nate had established a rapport with Ramón after he'd taken the doctor's first class. "There's nothing to say. They live their life. I live mine."

"Perry Stanton isn't someone you can ignore."

How true that was, Nate thought. Perry Stanton was one of the highest-paid older men of the cinema. As Nate was growing up, he and his mother had traveled with his dad from venue to venue, hoping for that big break. When it had come, Perry had landed a lead in a Broadway show. After that they'd moved to L.A. All of it was so long ago now. Yet somehow it wasn't.

"You know, when I was growing up, we constantly moved from place to place and had plenty of ups and downs. Still, I thought Mom and Dad had the perfect marriage."

"No marriage is perfect. Why do you think I stay single?" Ramón asked with a sly smile.

Remembering the stories in the tabloids when the scandal about Perry Stanton, his long-ago affair and the resulting love-child had broken, Nate knew they'd been mostly true. "I just never knew my father was as deceitful as he was famous. I guess my mother didn't, either."

"You were young when they divorced, weren't you?" Ramón asked, remembering what Nate had once confided.

"Eleven. My dad was on location almost that whole year. When he returned home…" Nate shook his head and felt his stomach twist, remembering. "I never felt a silence so cold as the one between them. Six months later he'd moved out and my mother had given me the excuse that they'd grown apart. It was his career, she'd said. I was gullible enough to believe it."

"Back then you were thinking about becoming an actor yourself. You were in that family drama when your parents divorced."

"Yeah, I was," Nate replied. "During the year after Mom and I moved to Malibu, too. But after my parents' divorce, I realized I didn't want a career and a profession that could destroy a marriage. I was glad the series ended."

The two men stared at the palm trees and irrigated lawn behind Ramón's condo.

Ramón broke the silence. "When did you last see your folks?"

"I flew out for Christmas. I spent Christmas Eve with Mom and had dinner with Dad on Christmas day. But nothing's been the same since the scandal broke."

"You have to let your anger fade, Nate. They tried to protect you."

Protect him? They hadn't been honest with him.

Nate had thought his life had been planned out. He had been a partner in an L.A. veterinarian practice and was engaged to Linda Sheridan, a kindergarten teacher who had a five-year-old daughter. Then somehow the tabloids had gotten hold of the best-kept secret in L.A. Perry Stanton had been unfaithful to his wife. He had a second son he'd never acknowledged, Cole Patterson—age twenty-three, and sources claimed he'd paid off the child's mother handsomely.

"I'll never understand why actors are so newsworthy," Nate muttered. "They're just people like everyone else."

"They make a hell of a lot more money," Ramón reminded him.

"Still…" He shook his head. "They didn't only hound my parents. They camped out at the veterinary clinic *and* my apartment. I can't believe they went after Linda like they did. If only Kristi hadn't been in the middle of it that day."

Knowing Linda was Nate's fiancée, a group of reporters had tailed her, then confronted her when she was picking up Kristi at school. They had surrounded mother and daughter and scared them both to death. Linda had broken her engagement to Nate soon after, saying she didn't want her life to be part of a circus. He'd told her they would move somewhere else and no one had to know who he was. But she'd insisted her family and her life was in Los Angeles and that's where she wanted to stay. Now he realized she hadn't loved him enough to change her life. She hadn't loved him enough to work out whatever problems would crop up between them.

"Are you sorry you left L.A.?" Ramón asked.

"No. I've never looked back." The only reminder of his former life was the sports car under the tarp in his garage. He thought about his practice now…his new house…Brooke. "Sometime soon I'd like you to meet the doctor who's joined me."

"Maybe I'll have to drive up to Whisper Rock one of these days. I'm sure I can fit it in between my golf games." He looked down at Frisco. "Does this big fella like her?"

"Went right up to her as soon as he saw her."

"If she just arrived, I guess you haven't seen her in action, yet."

"Actually, I have." He told Ramón about Everett Mc-Coy's cow. "I swear she gave that cow something," he finished. "But she says she didn't."

Ramón looked at him thoughtfully. "I've read about vets who seem to communicate with animals."

"What do you mean…communicate?"

"I don't know how to explain it, exactly. They use their hands for diagnosis and so they can feel the hot and cold spots where there might be trouble. It has to do with energy and the like."

"What journals do *you* read?" Nate asked sardonically.

"I've always read a wide variety of materials. I try to keep an open mind."

Just then Nate's cell phone buzzed. "That's probably Brooke," he said to Ramón, as he took the phone from his jacket pocket.

An hour later Nate had picked up Brooke at her grandmother's ranch and they'd begun the drive north. She hadn't spoken much, and as he'd said goodbye to Granna, Cal Pennington and Tessa, he was aware of the tension vibrating in the small house.

Brooke had given her grandmother a heartfelt hug goodbye, then knelt in front of Tessa. He'd been surprised when she'd said, "I'll see you on Wednesday." When Tessa had held up her hand and asked, "How many?" Brooke had smiled and counted off the little girl's fingers. "Monday, Tuesday, Wednesday. Three days." Then she'd given her little sister a hug. To her dad, she'd simply said, "I'll be thinking good thoughts."

Now here they were, and Brooke had been silent ever since.

The change of scenery was gradual as they left the warmer climate and headed toward the mountains. Brooke's lavender scent, her natural beauty, drew his gaze every few miles. Finally Nate asked, ''Do you want to talk about it?''

When she shifted toward him, her eyes were troubled. ''I'm not sure you're going to be glad you hired me.''

''Why?''

''I'm going to bring Tessa back to Whisper Rock on Wednesday for a week or so.''

''Because of your dad's surgery?''

She nodded. ''He feels it will be too much for Granna to take care of him *and* Tessa while he's recuperating. But I think he has another motive, too.''

Nate just waited.

''He's making me Tessa's legal guardian, and he wants us to spend time together. I guess he's not just thinking about the surgery but the future, too. He said he wants us to get to know each other so that if the need arises, Tessa will already be comfortable with me.''

''Is this something you've discussed with him before?''

Her brow wrinkled, and she shook her head. ''I haven't seen my father in four years. Before that we didn't discuss anything. He was like a ghost…in and out of my life on a whim.''

''How does your mother fit into all of this?''

It was a few long moments until Brooke decided whether or not to answer. Then she said softly, ''She didn't want me. My father convinced her to keep me and give me to Granna. Neither of them wanted the responsibility of a child. A year after I was born, she caught pneumonia, didn't know it and didn't get to a doctor in time. After that my father moved to Hawaii…then France. He's been all over the world.''

"Is he independently wealthy?"

"Far from it. He's worked all kinds of jobs—from hotel manager to travel guide." She looked out at the scenery and then back at Nate. "I know I was supposed to start work officially on Monday, and I'd like to. Maybe while Tessa's with me I could bring her to the clinic?"

"It might work for a few hours," Nate said cautiously.

"I spent most of my time with her this afternoon, and she seems easily entertained. I could see patients while she colors or listens to books on tape. She seems to like that. I could check on her between patients." Brooke sighed, then decided, "No. I can't do that to her. Maybe I shouldn't officially start for another two weeks. This is like asking for a vacation as soon as I'm hired on. I am really sorry, Nate."

"Life happens," he said with a shrug. "Why don't I put you on part-time for the next two weeks. Ellie loves children. If you help her with some of the paperwork, she might be willing to watch Tessa for you while you see patients. You can look in on her between them."

"I don't know how to thank you," Brooke said with so much feeling, Nate felt as if he'd just handed her the world.

"I've been handling the practice on my own for three years, Brooke. Having you around at all will be a relief."

Her gaze met his for that brief moment of shaking awareness that brought their kiss into his mind. He remembered everything about it...how she'd felt in his arms...how she'd tasted...how she'd responded.

Breaking eye contact, he concentrated on the ribbon of road before him and the rest of the drive.

Brooke watched the high desert landscape transform into pine trees and patches of snow. She was still reeling from the awesome responsibility of being legal guardian for her half sister. For her *sister,* she corrected herself. Little Tessa had already stolen a corner of her heart, and she was actually looking forward to taking care of her for a week. Yet her father's assumption that she would do it without protest bothered her, as well as all the unresolved feelings she felt toward him.

Nate was being so kind and understanding about all of it that she wondered if he was a different caliber of man than she had met before—a different caliber of man from her father and Tim. Maybe he could understand her gift and why she had to move from place to place. Yet helping her readjust her schedule for the next couple of weeks was more than a stone's throw away of accepting something she still didn't completely understand herself.

The last rays of light were trailing across the clinic's parking lot as Nate pulled in. Brooke spotted someone on the porch. It was a little girl, and she was holding something in her arms.

"It looks as if you have a visitor," Brooke said as he turned off the ignition.

"That's Jenny Warner. She and her family live two properties down."

Nate hopped out and let Frisco out behind him. The dog ran to the grove of trees beside the clinic as Nate met Brooke on the porch where Jenny sat on the bench, her arms filled with a blanket and something wrapped in it.

"Hi, Jenny," Nate said with a smile as he hunkered down before her. "It's cold for you to be sitting out here."

"I haven't been here long. Mom said I could see if you were home. When you weren't, I decided to wait a little."

Brooke crouched down beside Jenny, too, and under the clinic's porch light saw that the little girl appeared to be about ten. She was bundled up in a red-and-yellow down parka with a red ski cap on her head. A fringe of light-brown bangs dipped over her brows. "Hi, Jenny, I'm Brooke. I'm helping Dr. Nate now. What have you got?"

Jenny pulled back the blanket to reveal a pure-white kitten that looked to be about eight weeks old. "I found her in our backyard this morning. Mom says I can't keep her because we already have two cats and a dog. I took care of her in the garage most of the day. But she's sick. That's why I brought her to you. Can you make her better and find her a good home?"

There was so much hopeful expectancy in Jenny's eyes that Brooke didn't even take time to consult with Nate. The kitten sneezed, and Brooke could see that she indeed was sick, with an upper respiratory infection.

She gathered up the animal into her hands and held the kitten close to her chest. "Let's take her inside and examine her."

Nate stood, straightened and took out his keys. As he unlocked the clinic door, he glanced appraisingly at Brooke and the kitten.

After Jenny pushed her hand into the pocket of her jacket, she pulled out a handful of crumpled bills. "I saved up my allowance from chores. Mom said it would cost money to bring her here."

"We'll talk about settling up after we see what we can do for her," Nate decided.

Brooke liked Nate more each day. She knew he wasn't going to charge Jenny for being kind to a stray animal.

He said to Brooke, "Any one of the exam rooms is okay. I'm going to whistle for Frisco."

Having familiarized herself with the offices and the exam rooms, Brooke now grabbed a clean towel from a cupboard and laid it on the table in exam room two. Then she carefully set down the little white fur ball. It meowed up at her and then sneezed again.

"You are having a time of it," Brooke said gently, as she took a stethoscope from the counter and gently examined the kitten. After a few moments she stuck the stethoscope into a drawer and held the kitten in her hands. This was one sick little animal.

When Nate entered the room, there was a woman behind him. She was only about five feet tall, with light-brown, curly hair and tortoiseshell glasses. Nate introduced Brooke. "This is Jenny's mom."

Dorothy Warner shook her head. "I didn't want Jenny out in this cold any longer, so I drove down to pick her up. You ready to go home, honey?"

"I don't know." Jenny looked up at Brooke. "Can you make her better?"

"You told them we can't keep her, right?" her mother reminded her.

"Yes, Mom. I told her."

As she spoke, Brooke kept her hands on the kitten, gently rubbing her fingers over its fur. "I'll do my best."

"Can I come visit her?" Jenny asked.

"Sure you can. But it might take a couple of days until she feels better."

"That's okay. I'll come after school on Tuesday."

"That'll be fine."

Dorothy draped her arm around Jenny's shoulders. "I wish we could keep another cat, but we just can't."

After Jenny's mom had herded her daughter out of the office and Nate heard the clinic door close, he eyed Brooke skeptically. "You might be fighting a losing battle. That kitten is pretty sick. I don't even have to go over her myself to see that. And the recurrence rate in respiratory infections in kittens—"

"I know what the statistics say, but I don't believe in statistics."

"Brooke…"

"Nate, I discussed my methods of treatment with you during our interview. I do whatever I can, including holistic remedies. I'm going to start her on an antibiotic because I'm afraid we'll lose her to a secondary infection if I don't. But in the meantime I'm going to build up her immune system any way I know how. In cases like these, I've seen wonderful results when the kitten is put on the right diet with vitamin and mineral supplements."

"She's a stray, Brooke."

"Yes, she is. And she'll make someone a wonderful pet if they know how to take care of her."

The kitten was wheezing, and Brooke didn't want to waste any time. She opened the bottom cupboard door and pulled out a hot water bottle. Handing it to Nate she asked, "Would you fill this for me? About three-quarters full."

Nate gave her another skeptical glance but took the bottle and returned with it a few minutes later. She had already given the kitten her first dose of medicine. Brooke was intensely aware of Nate watching every move she made. As she took a paper grocery bag from a stack in the cupboard and turned down the top to make a collar around the outside, she asked him to put it in one of the cages along with a litter box.

"What's this for?" he asked as he looked at the bag.

"It'll make her feel safer in the big cage. She can crawl into it."

Nate's brows arched, but he took the bag into the area of the clinic where sick animals were housed. They didn't have any there at the moment.

Gathering up another clean towel along with the kitten,

Brooke spoke to the little animal gently as she carried her to the cage. After she asked Nate to wrap a towel around the hot-water bottle and place it inside the bag, she set the kitten inside with it. The little animal curled up on it and closed her eyes.

Frisco had trailed Nate inside and was now looking up at the cage with interest.

"He's good around other animals," Brooke said.

"Usually. He wants to be everybody's friend."

She smiled. "That's a good trait to have." After Brooke made sure the kitten was as comfortable as she could be, she said to Nate, "You don't have to stay."

He was standing very close to her. He had worn a denim shirt today, and it was open at the throat. Black hair curled in the vee, and the feel of his lips on hers became a vivid memory that brought heat to her cheeks.

"What else are you going to do for her?" he asked, his voice husky.

She suddenly knew that if he stayed, they'd kiss again. She didn't want that. She didn't want to risk losing her heart. And it would be a risk, once Nate knew why she moved from place to place...why she might not stay in Whisper Rock.

Seizing upon a practical answer, she replied, "I'm going to mix vitamins with some of the prescription food I brought along and see if she'll take it. I'm hoping I can get her to drink, too."

"Brooke, she's very sick," he gently said again.

"I know she is. But I've seen kittens turn around before. I have to try."

Stepping away from the cage, he nodded to the far wall. "There's a small light over there I leave on when we have animals here. Just lock up when you leave."

When Nate exited the room, Brooke breathed a sigh of

relief. It would be too easy to get close to him. Thank goodness she had something else to concentrate on tonight besides her father's operation…her beginning affection to Tessa…her attraction to Nate.

Unable to help herself, she reached inside the cage and lifted out the little bundle of white fur, cuddling her close. The kitten looked up at her with innocent eyes, then rubbed her chin against Brooke's finger.

"I think I'm going to name you Angel," Brooke whispered, and felt tears prick in her eyes as the day caught up with her. Then she took a deep breath and settled Angel into her cozy nest once more.

Nate was using an air mattress under his bedroll and had been comfortable the past few nights on the floor. His furniture would be arriving tomorrow. If he finished staining the wood molding, he could really put his house in order.

Sitting up, he glanced at the clock by his side and saw it was 3:00 a.m. It was as if the emptiness of the house had awakened him. Strange. He was usually a sound sleeper. Climbing to his feet, he yawned, stretched and went to the window that looked out of the master suite over toward the clinic. There were lights on there!

His gaze automatically went to Brooke's apartment and he saw a light there, too, glowing in her kitchen. Had she forgotten to turn out the lights in the clinic, or was she still up? If she was still up, maybe she needed his help.

Watch out, Stanton, he told himself as he went to the closet and pulled out a pair of jeans and a shirt. He'd almost kissed her again earlier, and that would have been a mistake. Brooke seemed as open and natural as a woman could be. But she had a lot on her plate right now with her dad's surgery and taking care of her sister. He also sensed that Brooke had secrets. He didn't want to get involved in secrets and someone else's drama. He'd had enough drama to last him for the next century.

After he quickly dressed, he went downstairs and grabbed his coat from one of the pegs he'd installed on the kitchen wall. The night was silent as he stepped outside, and the light from the clinic beckoned to him.

He found the door unlocked, and when he went inside, he called, "Brooke?"

"In here," she called back.

Her voice had come from her office, and he headed that way. When he stepped inside, he noticed that she'd changed clothes. She was wearing a turquoise sweatsuit that looked warm and comfortable. Bright-red embroidery trimmed the shoulders and the front. She was sitting in the high-back desk chair, a fluffy towel on her lap. The white kitten was curled on the towel, and Brooke held the little animal's head in her hands, her thumbs on the kitten's face.

"What are you doing?" he asked gruffly, the sight of her caring for the tiny animal touching him.

"I came down to check on her. She's so stuffy and having trouble breathing. So I've been doing acupressure."

"Is it helping?"

"It's relaxing her. She seems to be breathing more easily."

He came over and crouched down beside the chair so he could see exactly what Brooke was doing. "Are you going to stay up all night with her?"

"I will if it helps Angel feel better."

Looking up at Brooke, he saw the caring on her face. "I think you're getting attached."

"I think I am, too."

She didn't look away, and he felt he was getting to know everything important about Brooke by gazing into her honest brown eyes. "If you take her up to your apartment, you can both rest more comfortably."

"If I take her up to my apartment, I'll want to keep her."

He rose to his feet. "You could."

Brooke's thumbs gently slid over the kitten's cheeks. "I haven't had a pet since I was a child. It just didn't seem...practical."

"Sometimes we can't live our lives practically."

Her gaze met his again. "You sound as if you know about that."

"I know I thought I had my life planned, and then everything changed. Now I try not to count on plans." When Brooke's gaze didn't waver, he saw a knowing there...as if she understood exactly what he meant. There was so much about this woman that got to him on a very deep level. "So you've named her Angel?"

"It seemed to fit." Brooke's long lashes fluttered downward, and she lifted Angel closer to her breasts. "Do you mind if I have a kitten in the apartment?"

The kitten cuddled against Brooke, and he felt himself become aroused. "Frisco had the run of the place. I think there's plenty of room for you and a kitten."

When Brooke smiled at him then, it was the most beautiful smile he had ever seen. It stirred up feelings in him— of desire and tenderness—that he couldn't deny. Bending his head to her, he pressed a firm, long, heartfelt kiss onto her lips. She responded by lightly parting hers. But he didn't take the kiss further. He knew better. He knew himself well enough, that if he did, he'd want to carry her up to her apartment and do more than kiss her. Neither of them were ready for that.

Blazes! He'd known her for less than a week.

Straightening, he couldn't remember the last time a chaste kiss like that had aroused him so much. "I'll see you in the morning," he said huskily, searching her face to see if she'd been as affected as he was.

"In the morning," she murmured, then ducked her head and turned her attention back to Angel.

As Nate left the clinic a few moments later, he felt as if his world had suddenly tilted and his well-planned life had taken a detour once again.

Chapter Four

The following day, darkness had fallen by the time Nate said goodbye to Mrs. Ginnehy and her Chihuahua.

Brooke came through the door from the kennel area and saw him. Smiling, she asked, "How did you handle all of this on your own?"

He and Brooke had been seeing patients steadily all day, except for the half hour he'd taken to let delivery men bring appliances and furniture into his house. "I put in seventy hours some weeks. That's why I need assistance if I want a life." He checked his watch. "Are you going to go up to your apartment to get something for supper?"

"That...and to check on Angel," she admitted.

A look of tenderness was in her eyes, and he felt drawn again to it...and *her*. "I noticed she wasn't in her cage this morning, and I figured you'd taken her along. How's she doing?"

As if Brooke was drawn to him, too, she took a few steps closer. "She's sleeping a lot, but she's eating and drinking, and that's a good sign." Suddenly Brooke yawned and smiled sheepishly. "Maybe we'll both get some sleep tonight."

Sleep, a bed, Brooke… For a moment his imagination and baser urges took over. Suddenly the cell phone on his belt beeped. Restraining his thoughts and his urges, he said, "Excuse me a minute." Pressing the button, he answered the call. "Stanton here."

"Nate, do you have a few minutes?"

His father never introduced himself because he needed no introduction. "Just a few." To Brooke he said, "I'm going to take this in my office."

She nodded. "I'm going to run upstairs. I won't be too long. I want to go over the surgery schedule for tomorrow."

As he watched Brooke go to her office for her coat, he thought about their kiss last night—the kiss that had been brief but potent, chaste yet arousing.

"Nate, are you there?"

He had almost forgotten about his father. All of his other concerns seemed to evaporate whenever Brooke was around. "I'm here, Dad. I just wanted to go into my office. What's up?"

"What are you doing the first weekend in February?"

"I'm not sure yet," Nate answered cautiously.

"Can you clear your schedule and fly out here?"

Fly back to Los Angeles. He had no desire to return anytime soon. "This really isn't the time of year for me to take a vacation. What's going on?"

"I'm hosting a telethon. It's a fund-raiser to expand a pediatrics ward for cancer treatment. I've got some big talent. I thought you might enjoy it."

"I don't think so, Dad. I've taken on a new associate and I'm trying to adjust to that."

There were a few moments of awkward silence. That awkwardness had begun after the scandal had broken and had stayed with them. Finally Perry Stanton offered, "A new associate's just what you need. Whoever it is should be able to cover for you."

Nate rubbed the back of his neck. "We haven't worked all of that out yet. It's complicated. She's going to be taking care of her little sister for a while, and she might not be able to cover."

"So it's a woman, is it? Is she pretty?"

Closing his eyes, Nate counted to ten. "Whether she is or not has nothing to do with what kind of vet she'll be."

"I suppose not. I was just hoping she'd capture your interest. Your mother and I would like some grandchildren before we're too old to care."

"Maybe your other son could do that for you," Nate said, without the bitterness he'd felt three years ago, but still with a tinge of rancor.

The dead silence that fell between them this time seemed to vibrate with hurt, anger and regret. His father broke it. "Cole is pursuing his law career. He's been hired by a firm that handles entertainment contracts."

Curious in spite of himself, Nate asked, "Which firm is he with?"

There was a pause. "Conroy, Matheson and James."

"The attorneys you use to negotiate *your* contracts?" Nate asked, sensing what was coming.

"Yes. I recommended him. But they hired him on his own merit."

"Whether they did or not is none of my business," Nate said with a sigh. "Look, Dad. February won't work."

His father must have heard the certainty in his voice.

"That's a shame. I was looking forward to seeing you again. We didn't have much time at Christmas."

"Maybe in the spring."

"Yes, maybe in the spring. Keep in touch and let me know how that partner works out."

"She's not a partner, but I'm hoping she'll become one. I could use the capital to expand."

"If you need money…"

Nate was sorry he'd said anything. "No, I don't. I'm doing well. I'd just like to build up the clinic."

"Are you going to send me pictures of the new house?"

Did his father really want to see it? "Sure. The furniture and appliances were just delivered today. Once I get it arranged, I'll photograph it."

"You take care of yourself, son. And give me a call now and then."

When Nate switched off the phone, his chest was tight with the turmoil he still felt about his parents and the secret they'd kept.

A few minutes later Nate was sitting at his desk going over the conversation again in his head when Brooke peeked in. "Aren't you going to have supper before evening hours begin?"

He plowed his hand through his hair. "I'm not hungry."

Taking another, closer look at him, Brooke stepped into his office. "Because of your call?"

He debated with himself, then admitted, "That was my father. Things have been a bit bumpy between us since I came out here."

Brushing her hair from her cheek, she tucked it behind her ear. "I understand bumpy."

Although Nate had never talked with anyone but

Ramón about what had happened, he realized he might have opened this conversation with Brooke because she *would* understand. "No one in Whisper Rock knows who my father is," Nate confessed.

Receptive to whatever he wanted to tell her, Brooke simply stood there.

"Have you ever heard of Perry Stanton?"

Her eyes grew wide. "The actor?"

"The one and only."

Her gaze considered him critically. "*That's* why you look familiar. Your hair waves like his across your forehead. And didn't I read you were in a TV show of your own?"

"Just for two years. Then the show went off the air, and I decided acting wasn't what I wanted to do with my life."

"I remember now," she said quietly. "A few years ago a big story broke about Perry Stanton's love child—" She stopped and her face reddened. "I'm sorry. I guess I was as interested as everyone else."

Nate grimaced. "The curiosity is natural, I suppose. Unfortunately, Dad did a few talk shows, too, hoping to give his side of it. But it only made the frenzy worse. That's why I left and came here."

"It sounds as if you needed the anonymity," she responded perceptively.

"I wanted a life that didn't have Perry Stanton stamped all over it. He hit it big when I was around seven. After that, everything in my life revolved around him. I can't tell you how great it's been to be out here and know someone wants to be my friend because of who I am, not because of who my father is. I also wanted a simpler life. I have that here. Everything is uncomplicated. There are no smoke or mirrors, no spin doctors, no reporters around every corner, though John Warner *does* live down the street. Jenny's father works for the *Whisper Rock Chronicle*. Thank goodness Stanton's a common enough name that no one associates me with my dad. As long as I keep a low profile, I don't have to worry about anyone finding out." His gaze met hers, and he suddenly realized what valuable information he'd just put in her hands.

She must have realized it, too. "Don't worry, Nate. I understand. I'll never say anything to anyone."

He couldn't believe he'd only known her for a few days and he trusted her. With Brooke giving her word, he believed she could keep the secret. She was that kind of woman. He felt once more the sizzling attraction that had invaded every one of his encounters with her. "Enough about my life," he said with a quick grin. "How do you like working here?"

"I think I'm going to like it…a lot."

"Then why don't you think about—"

Holding up her hand to stop him, she asked, "Not now, okay? Can we table that discussion for…at least another month?"

He stood and approached her. "In a month, do you think anything's going to be different?"

"In a month, I might know where my father and my sister fit into my life. The time will give me a better feel for the people here."

Her hair escaped the push she'd given it behind her ear. A few wavy strands whispered along her cheek, and he fought the urge to finger them. "Don't you think people are essentially the same everywhere?"

She thought about that. "Maybe. But some are more open-minded than others. I'm hoping that's the case in Whisper Rock."

"As long as you treat their animals with the respect

and care I've seen you give them, you're not going to have any problems.''

When her face clouded, he wished she'd confide in him. He wished she'd tell him whatever it was that kept her moving.

Knowing the situation with her family, he thought about the rest of the week. ''I know you'll be gone all day Wednesday. I'll see patients on Thursday, and I won't schedule you for appointments on Friday, either.''

''I'd like to take all day Thursday with Tessa and ease her into being with me. Maybe Friday afternoon I could see a few patients again. I don't want to leave you in the lurch.''

''We'll play it by ear.''

She looked chagrined as she tilted her head. ''I have one more favor to ask. Can you look in on Angel on Wednesday and give her food, water and medicine? Pet her a little?''

He smiled, because he knew that Brooke considered the affection as important as the food and water. ''Sure, I'll check on her.''

Suddenly Brooke appeared very vulnerable. She was facing major disruption in her life so soon after her move, and that couldn't be easy. ''Everything's going to be all right.''

A glisten of tears suddenly shone in her eyes. ''I'm afraid something's going to happen to my father before I ever get to know him. I'm afraid Tessa won't want to be with me…that she'll be afraid so far from Granna and her dad.''

''She won't be afraid with you,'' Nate assured her. ''Nobody could be afraid with you.''

At his words Brooke seemed surprised.

Instead of kissing her as he wanted to do, he simply

put his arms around her and gave her the hug she seemed to need. The sweetness of lavender, the softness of her skin, the silkiness of her hair were temptations he resisted. But it was damn hard to do it.

"It'll be okay, Brooke. All of it. You'll see."

He hoped his words foretold the future. Because if they didn't, she'd be gone again, and he'd hardly ever know she'd touched his life.

When Brooke pulled up in front of the clinic on Wednesday night, she was bone tired and emotionally drained. She could have made the drive tomorrow morning, but she knew her grandmother was tired, too. If she and Tessa had stayed in Phoenix, Granna would have tried to take care of their every need in spite of her own fatigue.

Looking over her shoulder, Brooke saw Tessa sleeping in the car seat in the back, the calico-print rag doll Granna had made tucked under her arm. She'd been quiet all day, and Brooke had kept close whenever she was around her, hoping her mere presence would reassure Tessa.

Suddenly a tall figure appeared in front of her van, and Brooke's breath hitched. Then she realized it was Nate. He must have been working at the clinic.

Coming over to her door, he waited until she opened it. "How did it go?" he asked, without preamble or niceties or small talk.

"Dad's in stable condition in intensive care. He has to lie flat for two days. Then if all goes well…they'll talk about releasing him."

After another look at Tessa, she climbed out of the van. "She fell asleep practically as soon as I started driving."

"Do you want me to carry her upstairs for you?"

"That would be great! Then I don't have to wake her."

Nate went around to the other side of the van, opened

the sliding door and unfastened the car seat's buckle. A few moments later he'd scooped Tessa and her doll into his arms and was striding toward the steps.

Brooke kept pace with him, Tessa's small suitcase in her grip. "You did that expertly."

"I've had to do it a few times before."

Brooke stopped for a moment, but Nate kept going. She ran to catch up.

Inside the apartment the kitchen light was glowing. Brooke appreciated the homelike beacon, and knew Nate had left it lit when he stopped in to check on Angel. The kitten was sleeping on a towel in a cardboard box Brooke had fashioned into a bed, one side lower than the other three, which had been left high to keep out drafts.

The kitten stretched, looked up at Brooke and meowed.

"It's good to see you, too," Brooke said, her voice low as she turned back the covers for Tessa, and Nate laid her gently in the bed.

As Brooke set Tessa's doll beside the pillow and then removed Tessa's coat and shoes, Nate scooped Angel into his hand and petted her. He said, "Jenny stopped by after school. I let her hold Angel."

"Jenny's a sweet girl, and she really loves animals. Last evening when she visited Angel, she told me all about her mom's dog, Biscuit, and their other pets."

Brooke was attempting to take off Tessa's overalls without jostling her too much when the little girl's eyes opened. "Bwooke?"

"Hi, honey. We're at my apartment, and you're in my bed. Let's just get these overalls off and you can go back to sleep."

But Tessa wasn't concerned about her clothes. Her little arms went around Brooke's neck. "Don't go."

Brooke hugged her tight. "I won't. I'm going to be

right here, sleeping beside you. We have another room-mate, too." She pointed to the white kitten in Nate's hands. "Her name is Angel."

Tessa's worried expression changed and she smiled. "A kittee! She your kittee?"

"I think she's going to be. She's sick. But I'm hoping we can make her all better."

"Like Daddy's sick?" Tessa asked somberly.

"Something like that."

"Pet her?" Tessa asked.

After Nate set the kitten in Tessa's lap, Tessa lay back on the pillows, and Angel settled in while the little girl stroked her.

Brooke couldn't keep from brushing Tessa's hair along her cheek. As Tessa's eyes began to close again, Brooke placed a kiss on her forehead. She'd discovered today that she loved her little sister. There wasn't an ounce of re-sentment left. Not toward Tessa. Her feelings toward her father might still be unresolved, but Tessa was a gift, the sister she'd never had, a connection she'd always wanted.

Looking up at Nate, she smiled. "I never knew I could feel so much love or tenderness toward a child. I guess this is how a mother feels."

Tessa was sleeping again, and Angel was purring. Nate held out his hand to Brooke to help her up. She didn't even hesitate to take it.

Walking over to the kitchen with her, he kept his voice low. "Do you have everything you need?"

Suddenly she knew she didn't. She needed him. It was a startling revelation because she considered herself self-sufficient. But being with Nate felt so right. She'd known him less than a week and already she was...

Falling in love with him!

The thought almost stopped her heart. She couldn't let

that happen, could she? Would she be able to stay in Whisper Rock? Wouldn't he eventually turn his back on her as her father had? As Tim had?

Nate must have seen the questions in her eyes. "If you do need anything, you have my number. Don't think about anything tonight except getting some sleep," he advised.

"Thank you, Nate."

He shook his head. "There's nothing to thank me for. I'll probably see you around tomorrow. If you want, bring Tessa in and we'll get her used to the animals."

Lifting her hand into his, he intertwined their fingers. When he gazed down at her, he said, "It seems as if I've known you a lot longer than a week."

"I feel that way, too." She should know better than to depend on Nate...to give into feelings that would eventually hurt her.

Yet when Nate's lips found hers, Brooke felt as if she'd come home. The fire of his desire heated her until she parted her lips and his tongue swept inside. They couldn't seem to get enough of the kiss or the moment, and she found herself wrapping her arms around him, letting him pull her tight against him so she could feel his arousal.

But both of them were aware of Tessa sleeping only ten feet away. Nate broke the kiss and put some distance between them. Brooke took a deep breath and tried to right her world. As he brushed his thumb down her cheek, he gave her a smile that made her melt inside. She didn't speak as he crossed to the door. When he left, he didn't say good-night.

After she locked the door and switched off the kitchen light, she went over to the bed and undressed, thinking of Nate, fearing and yet hoping what he could mean to her life.

* * *

The following morning when Brooke awakened, it was snowing—big, fat flakes that looked as if they meant serious business. Tessa stirred beside her in the bed, and Brooke looked down at her sleeping sister, a warm feeling stealing over her heart. Tessa had stayed close all night, cuddled against her. Brooke felt protective of her.

She noticed Angel was curled on the covers down by Tessa's feet, and she had to smile. Instead of being a burden, caring for Tessa was filling her heart with joy. Taking the phone from the nightstand, she glanced at the number she'd written on the notepad there, then dialed it. A few minutes later she'd learned her father was stable and doing well. Relief swept over her.

When she felt a tug on the sleeve of her nightshirt, she turned.

Tessa looked up at her and pushed her dark hair away from her eyes. "Hung'y." She pointed to the white kitten. "Angel hung'y, too."

Brooke laughed. "Well then, I guess I'll have to see what I can make for both of you. What would you like to do this morning? Color? Go get groceries? I'm going to have to do that sometime today."

The snow suddenly caught Tessa's attention, and she scrambled out of bed and scampered over to the window. "Play there," she said with a wide grin.

"I suppose we can for a little while. We'll have to bundle you up."

Tessa looked toward the bed and the kitten. "Angel, too?"

"No, I think Angel better stay inside." When Tessa's face fell, Brooke had another idea. "But I'll bet Frisco might like to play with us. We could ask Dr. Nate after breakfast. What do you think?"

With her forefinger in her mouth, Tessa thought about it for a minute, then she nodded vigorously.

An hour later, when Brooke took Tessa into the clinic, the three-year-old stayed close by Brooke's side. But as soon as Nate brought Frisco into the waiting area, she was all smiles.

Frisco held out his paw to her and she giggled.

Nate said, "You take good care of him." Assuring him that she would, Tessa nodded. To Brooke he advised, "Play in the fenced-in yard and make sure the gate is latched."

"You're sure this is okay?"

"Frisco will love cavorting in the snow with the two of you." Brooke saw the look in Nate's eyes that said he'd enjoy it, too. What would happen if she told Nate why she moved from place to place? If she told him a reporter had written an article about her two years ago? If she told him why she'd become a veterinarian? Then she remembered Tim's reaction and knew she was wishing for the impossible.

After an hour in the snow, Tessa's cheeks were red, and snow matted Frisco's tail and paws. Brooke took them up to her apartment, not sure what the kitten would do when she saw the big dog. After Frisco snuffled at her, she didn't seem intimidated, and he sat down beside Angel as if he'd made a new friend.

Once Brooke had toweled off the big dog, she made tomato soup and grilled-cheese sandwiches for lunch. They were just finishing when she heard Nate coming up the steps. She knew the sound of him already, and her pulse raced faster.

When she opened the door, he took in the scene and smiled. Frisco was sitting at Tessa's feet as she finished the last of her soup. Angel was curled on the bed, asleep.

"I think I've lost my dog," he joked.

"We're just enjoying his company," Brooke said teasingly. "Did you eat lunch? Want some soup?"

"Ellie brought in doughnuts this morning. I had one too many. I'm going to skip lunch. I closed the clinic. There's about four inches of snow out there already, and I need to go stock up on groceries. Do you need anything?"

"Do you mind if we come along? I want to let Tessa pick out some things she likes."

"That's fine. But I think we'd better get going. Sleet is on its way and that's going to make the roads treacherous."

The phone in the apartment rang, and Brooke said, "I'd better get that. It might be about my father."

When she picked up the receiver and said hello, she was shocked at the voice she heard.

"Hi, Brooke. It's been a long time."

Tim! She gasped and took a quick glance at Nate. "How did you find me?" she asked a bit shakily.

"That wasn't hard. I had mail forwarded to you in Syracuse, remember? When I phoned there your landlady gave me this number."

Brooke had called and given her former apartment manager the number here for emergencies only. "This must be important if you talked her into giving it to you."

"She was a hard sell, but charm goes a long way."

Unfortunately, Brooke knew Tim had plenty of charm. On top of that, he could read people well. "Why did you track me down?

"I had an interesting call from the *Chicago Tribune*."

"Oh?" She tried to keep the concern from her voice.

"It was a reporter who came across that article written about you. He was doing some kind of series on alternative medicine. Since I was mentioned, and I'm pretty visible, he contacted me to get hold of you.''

Tim made sure he moved in the correct social circles with the power brokers who could do the most for his law career. She knew he had political ambitions. ''What did you tell him?'' she asked, her voice hoarse.

''That I didn't know where you were, but I could probably find out. I thought I should check it out with you first.'' He paused. ''I felt badly about the way everything ended between us...why you left...the way you ran scared. You could use publicity with the *Tribune* to your advantage, turn what you do into a profitable enterprise.''

''That's not what I want.''

When he was silent, she said, ''Please don't tell him how he can reach me.''

''It would be a feature article, Brooke. You could explain everything.''

That was the problem. She couldn't explain it. ''No, thanks.''

''All right. If that's what you want. But if you change your mind, you know where to find me.''

When she hung up the phone, her hands were trembling and her palms were sweaty. Wiping them on her jeans, she turned toward the kitchen and saw that Nate had pulled out a chair and was sitting and watching her carefully.

''Was it news about your dad?'' he asked as a lead-in.

''No, it wasn't.''

''Do you want to tell me what it was about?'' His tone was casual but his intent wasn't.

''No.''

''Why not, Brooke? What are you running from?''

She could tell Nate now. She could tell him all of it. But if she did, he might not want her working with him.

He might tell her Whisper Rock wasn't the place for her.
"It's really none of your concern."

He was on his feet and close to her in an instant. "It
is my concern if someone's trying to hurt you. Who was
that on the phone?"

"It was…it was a man I was involved with a long time
ago."

"And what did he want?" There was a deep intensity
in Nate's eyes, almost possessive in its nature.

"He just wanted to let me know about an…opportunity
that had come up. But I'm not interested, and that's all
there was to it."

Nate searched her face. "Were you in an abusive relationship?" he asked pointedly.

"No!"

"This man doesn't want to find you? Get you back?"

"No, Nate. It's nothing like that. Honestly."

"Then tell me what it is," he said huskily.

She thought about what had happened with Tim…the
way he had looked at her after she'd tried to explain everything to him.

Tessa's spoon clattered in her bowl, and Brooke came
back to reality with a jolt. Nate might be a kind, understanding man, but understanding only went so far. If she
wanted to stay here in Whisper Rock, if she wanted to
practice with him, she'd have to take one risk at a time.
Telling him everything about herself was the last risk she
wanted to take. "We'd better go get those groceries before the roads get too slick."

"Why can't you trust me?" he asked.

"Because we've only known each other a week. Because trust isn't something I know much about." Slipping
away from him, she went to the table and carried the
dishes to the sink. If Nate kept pushing, she didn't know

what she was going to tell him. Or what she was going to do.

And if Tim didn't keep his promise? If he gave her location to that reporter?

Then Nate would know much more about her than he might ever want to know.

Chapter Five

When Nate transferred Tessa's seat to the back of his SUV, she looked as happy as the proverbial clam as she sat beside Frisco on the way to the grocery store. Nate, on the other hand, was on edge. Glancing at Brooke, he saw she was steadfastly staring out the windshield.

Tension built between them as sleet pinged and snow splattered on the windshield. He drove with care, more determined than ever to unravel the mystery that was Brooke Pennington.

If an abusive ex-husband or an abusive fiancé wasn't chasing her, what had made her run? What made it difficult for her to trust? The way she'd been abandoned as a child, certainly. But there was more to it than that. He was sure of it.

The grocery store's neon lights blinked at them through the snow and sleet. "We'll make this fast," he said. "Four-wheel drive or not, the roads are getting treacherous."

"Are you going to leave Frisco here?" Brooke asked as she unfastened her seatbelt."

"Yes. I'll put down the window a crack. He'll snatch up any snowflakes that manage to fly in."

Brooke gave Nate a smile that almost made him forget the conversation they'd had in her apartment. Or not had. She was wearing a turquoise knit cap and seemed unconcerned about whether or not it would mess up her hair. He'd already figured out that turquoise must be her favorite color. It suited her. It was bright and yet rich and deep.

When had he thought in those terms about a woman before?

"Watch your step when you get out. It's probably slippery," he warned, not understanding the feelings for her that seemed to grow more intense every day. "I'll carry Tessa," he added. "Then we won't have to worry about her falling."

As he took Tessa out of her car seat, he remembered Linda's little girl, Kristi. Unfastening Tessa, he lifted her up. She wrapped her arms around his neck as Kristi had done so many times. The old longing to have a family of his own twisted his gut.

When he joined Brooke in front of the store, she studied him for a few moments.

"What?" he asked, feeling self-conscious.

"You looked far away for a moment."

"Maybe I'm just worried about getting back home."

Although she accepted his explanation, they both knew the weather wasn't the cause of whatever emotion she'd caught reflected on his face.

Once inside the store, Tessa took hold of Brooke's hand, and Nate noticed her protectively wrap her fingers around Tessa's.

"Any word on your father?" Nate asked.

"I think he's doing well. I talked to Granna before lunch. She had just been at the hospital. He has to lie flat on his back until tomorrow. I'll check in again then."

Navigating their cart quickly through the aisles, Nate saw that Tessa almost had to skip to keep up. He swooped her up into his arms again and carried her, pushing the cart one-handed.

"You'd make a wonderful dad," Brooke mused as if she were thinking aloud.

"I almost was a dad. The woman I was engaged to had a little girl who was five."

Brooke didn't seem to know what to say to that. They were halfway down the aisle when she asked a bit hesitantly, "Did you break off the engagement or did she?"

The wheels on their cart squeaked. "She did."

The expression on Brooke's face said that she was absorbing that. But she didn't ask any more questions and he was grateful. It had been a long time since he'd thought about Linda and Kristi and everything that had happened. Dredging it up was never pleasant. It brought back too clearly the way he'd felt betrayed by Linda. The way he'd felt left out and removed from his own parents. Maybe that's why he empathized with Brooke's situation so well. Although it was obvious she had taken Tessa into her heart, she must still have resentment and anger toward her dad. He didn't even know what *his* half brother looked like. And he realized he had no desire to know. Brooke was definitely a bigger person than he was.

Like most children, Tessa pointed to goodies she'd like to have. He watched Brooke weigh the pros and cons of sugar-coated cereal and peanut-butter-stuffed cookies. But she gave in more than she didn't, adding granola bars to the basket, too, though. When they were checking out, Tessa pointed to a candy bar.

Nate leaned close to Brooke and murmured, "This is a special time for both of you. It's okay to indulge." He could smell her sweet scent…see the few, very light freckles on her cheeks.

As she turned toward him slightly, her lips almost brushed his jaw. He sensed her quick intake of breath. Recovering, she whispered, "I haven't indulged myself in a long time."

He knew she was talking about more than candy bars, and he wished they were alone in his bedroom in the dark so he could really teach her about indulging. "Then it's time," he said with certainty.

Plucking three candy bars from the box, he set them with their groceries. When Tessa smiled at him, he gave her a conspiratorial wink.

A short time later, Frisco barked as Brooke watched Nate turn up his jacket collar against the needles of sleet and load the groceries into the SUV that was now encased in ice. As Brooke made sure Tessa was secure in her seat, she was still thinking about Tim's call and Nate's reaction. How she wished she could confide in him!

In the car they drove silently until they were about halfway to the clinic. Nate muttered, "We've got trouble."

Brooke looked up ahead expecting to see a fender-bender or traffic backed up because someone was stuck. But she didn't see either. "What's wrong?"

He gestured to the houses along the side of the street. "Not one light is on. Don't you think that's odd?"

Late-afternoon shadows looked almost like dusk with the snow and the dark clouds. Soon it would be dark. "Do you think the electricity went out?"

"That would be my guess. I'm glad I decided to build a fireplace in the house."

"Does the clinic have a generator?"

"Not yet. That was next on my list. Fortunately, we're not boarding any animals right now."

Considering what would be best for Tessa, she went over their options. "Maybe I should go to a motel in Flagstaff. I could sneak Angel in."

"Brooke." There was an exasperated note in Nate's voice. "Do you think I'd let you drive into Flagstaff in this weather?"

"I can't keep Tessa in a cold apartment."

"Of course you can't. When we get back, you can gather up Angel and I'll light a fire in the fireplace. There's no telling how long the ice storm will last, so you'd better pack pj's for Tessa, too."

He wanted them to stay at *his* house? Fighting her attraction to him while working was difficult enough. Sitting in front of a fire… "We can't just barge in on you when we don't know how long we'll need to stay."

"I've got plenty of room. You and Tessa and Angel won't take up much."

She went silent at that, thinking how generous Nate was, how he didn't seem to mind having his life disrupted or his plans changed.

"Tessa will be a good chaperone if you're worried about me having ulterior motives," he added wryly.

Not worried about Nate's motives, she was concerned with her deepening feelings for him, the excited way he made her feel… "I was just wondering how I'm going to repay your generosity."

Casting a glance at her in the shadows, he grinned. "You can do that by figuring out how to cook us a meal over the fire."

Suddenly Tim's call seemed long ago and time with Nate too special to pass up. "That shouldn't be difficult. Besides, we can always have some of Tessa's cereal if we get desperate."

"I think I'd rather have another one of your vegetarian concoctions," he admitted wryly.

Ten minutes later Nate skidded to a stop in front of his garage, knowing he'd done the best thing by asking Brooke and Tessa to stay with him. He told himself his invitation was purely practical and had nothing to do with his attraction to her or the daddy-like feelings he experienced carrying Tessa. The sleet was heavy and thick now, and everything was iced.

He opened his door. "I have to go into the garage and put the door on manual."

"And I have to get Angel."

Shaking his head, he decided, "Those stairs are going to be slick. I'll get you and Tessa settled inside, and then I'll go get Angel."

"But I have to get some of Tessa's clothes and Angel's vitamins…"

"Make a list. Your apartment's not that big. I'm sure I can find everything."

When she didn't respond, he asked, "What's the matter?"

"I'm just used to taking care of myself. That's all."

Closing the door again, he couldn't help slipping his hand under Brooke's hair and rubbing his thumb along her cheek. "It's not so hard, Brooke. Just smile and say thank you." His tone was light and he meant it to be teasing.

But she was completely serious as she murmured, "Thank you."

Nate felt as if he'd done something significant…as if

maybe Brooke had given him a little bit of her trust along with the words.

She cleared her throat and pulled away. ''I'll make that list.''

After Nate took the groceries inside, lit a fire, found his camp stove and made sure Brooke and Tessa were comfortable in his living room, he went to Brooke's apartment and gathered up everything on her list, including a partial bag of cat litter. He had a dishpan in the basement Angel could use. The temperature had already dropped in Brooke's apartment. Before he put Angel in her carrier, he couldn't help examining her. She wasn't completely recovered, but she was certainly doing much better than when Jenny had brought her to the clinic.

The hot-water bottle was one of the items on Brooke's list. Filling it, he tucked it in with Angel before he started the icy trek back to the house. He always liked caring for animals, but he cared for them differently from Brooke. She treated them almost like children. She had such respect for them that he'd never seen in a vet before. He wished she would open up to him. He wished again she'd tell him her life history. Maybe she would if he pushed the process along. Maybe she would if he told her the reason he hadn't been involved with a woman for three years.

When he entered his house again, the temperature had dropped more there, too, at least in the kitchen. The fire he'd started in the living room was keeping that room warmer. Frisco usually came to meet him when he came in the door, but he didn't this time, and Nate soon saw why. Tessa was snuggled into a corner of his new sofa, a cover printed with a mountain scene thrown over her. Frisco lay stretched out on the rest of the sofa with his head in her lap. She was petting him and watching Brooke.

Before he'd gone to the apartment above the clinic, he'd set up the camp stove on the heavy pine coffee table. Brooke had it going now with a frying pan over one burner and a saucepan on the other. The aroma of food made Nate's stomach grumble, but the sight of her on her knees in her pink-and-white sweater and jeans, with her pretty hair falling down her back as she stirred whatever was in the pan, caused other parts of his body to get restless, too.

Setting the kitten and her carrier beside the sofa, he asked, "What's cooking?"

"Pan biscuits and a rice, kidney-bean and tomato concoction I hope you're going to like. If not, I guess you'll just have to spread peanut butter on your biscuits."

He chuckled. "I'll give whatever you make a try. It smells good, so it probably tastes good, too. I couldn't carry Angel's bed with the rest of the stuff. Do you think she'll sleep in her carrier?"

"Either there or on the sofa beside Frisco. Is he allowed up there?"

The couch was a durable material, a tight-woven, rust-and-green print that was stain resistant. Its huge pillows made it comfortable for lounging or sitting. "I bought furniture with both Frisco and me in mind. He's allowed as long as he doesn't have muddy paws."

"And the same goes for you?" she joked.

"The same goes for me."

When Nate unzipped the carrier, it took a few moments until Angel poked her head out. But then she saw Brooke at the stove and Tessa on the sofa. With a catch of her claws on the cover and another short leap, she was on

Tessa's lap, sitting by Frisco's nose. The dog raised his head, crossed his paws and set his nose on them again.

Nate was struck by the feeling of rightness in this scene. He couldn't remember ever feeling exactly like this with Linda. With her, everything was planned, expected, arranged. She'd been a scheduled, disciplined person who hadn't liked chaos. Not that he was fond of chaos, either, but he tried to roll with the punches. Linda hadn't been good at that. Her little girl's bedtime had been set in stone, as had her diet and mealtimes. He knew children needed stability, but they needed a sense of adventure, too. Brooke seemed comfortable with instilling that in Tessa.

"I still have the air mattress and sleeping bag I was using before my furniture arrived. I'll go get them. Anything else we might need?"

"A few blankets and pillows, maybe. By the time you get back this should be ready. How do granola bars sound for dessert?"

"Like we're on a backpacking trip. But I can stand it if we brew some coffee."

"Coffee for you, tea for me."

"I should have known," he mumbled, as he headed for the stairs for everything else they'd need to bunk in the living room for the night.

After supper, with coffee brewing on one burner and water warming for tea on the other, Brooke sat beside Nate on the sofa, Tessa stretched out on the floor, coloring. The animals alternately watched her and snoozed. The oil lamp on the end table gave off a mellow, yellow light that seemed to flicker up to the ceiling.

She'd enjoyed supper with Nate more than any dinner she'd ever had with Tim in a five-star restaurant. They'd talked about innovations in their field, made up rhymes to entertain Tessa and glanced at each other often. Brooke knew she was feeling too comfortable with him...feeling too much of everything. Yet she was enjoying it so much she couldn't seem to stop. Nate had turned on a battery-operated radio, and soft music played intermittently with weather reports as they waited to enjoy coffee or tea with their granola bars.

Nate was staring into the flames as if they could reveal all the secrets of life. How she wished they could.

At the scrambling noise at the other side of the coffee table, Brooke watched Tessa push the coloring book aside as she curled up in the sleeping bag. She'd had an unusual day today and no nap, which Granna had told Brooke she sometimes took. As Brooke watched her sister, Tessa's eyes drifted shut, and she hugged the rag doll Granna had made for her close to her little body.

"She's down for the count," Nate noted.

"I hope her dreams are as sweet as she is," Brooke said.

"Do you think she's worrying about her dad?"

"It's hard to tell. She asked me twice today when she was going back to Granna's. I know she misses him." Brooke could remember the missing she'd felt as a child, only she hadn't known when or if she'd see her dad again. Why couldn't he have stayed in Phoenix? Why had he chosen not to be a part of her life?

"Kids can teach us so much about ourselves," Nate murmured.

Since he'd brought up the subject, she pursued it. "You said you were engaged to someone who had a five-year-old?"

There was silence, and then he answered her. "Yes. Kristi was sunshine, just like Tessa is. I thought she was going to be my daughter. I thought I was going to be lucky enough to be an instant dad."

The next question came easily for Brooke because she wanted to know so badly. "What happened?"

"The scandal happened."

She faced him more squarely. "I don't understand. What did that have to do with your engagement?"

Leaning forward, Nate gazed into the flames again. "Family connections can't be kept in a sealed box unless you work really hard at it. When I met Linda at the symphony one evening, we began talking and realized we liked a lot of the same things—surfing, waterskiing, sailing. She knew who I was but didn't seem impressed by it, and I was glad of that. I'd dated women who only wanted to go out with me to meet my father, so Linda was refreshing."

He turned toward Brooke. "But after becoming engaged, I should have seen the signs that my feelings were deeper than hers, that she saw our relationship as practical and convenient and just another step forward in her life. To me, she and Kristi were becoming my world."

"I hear that's what you feel when you fall in love," Brooke said softly, so aware of the man beside her, the scent of his cologne, the strength of his arms that had been obvious in the way he'd carried Tessa.

"You've never made someone your world?" Nate asked.

Not wanting to be a mystery to Nate, she revealed, "I was working on it once. Then I found out…I found out the man I was seeing…his career and political ambitions were more important than any relationship." Knowing she couldn't give more than that, she turned the focus back to Nate. "You said the scandal was the reason for your broken engagement. Why? You hadn't done anything wrong."

"No, I hadn't. But I was involved. The reporters

wanted my side of what happened. They wanted to know if my father's relationship and his illegitimate child really had been a secret all these years...what my mother was feeling...if we were now estranged from my father...or if none of it made any difference. But I wasn't about to talk to them about any of it. They always twist things the way they want to see them...or the way their magazine wants to see them. They camped out outside my condo. But I was used to all of that. There had been times in my dad's career, and even for the short time I was involved in the business, that we had to deal with reporters en masse. We learned to use back entrances, disguises, security."

"You mean bodyguards?"

"Now and then." He leaned back into the sofa cushion. "The problem was—Linda wasn't used to dealing with any of it. When the reporters couldn't get to first base with me, they hounded her. A news crew followed her when she went to pick up Kristi at school. When Kristi came out, they surrounded them. Flashbulbs went off, camcorders went on. Kristi was scared to death. Linda told me she couldn't live her life in a fishbowl. I suggested we move, anywhere else, away from all of it. But she insisted her family and friends were in L.A., and she didn't want to change her life. Linda was like that. Change and flexibility were very hard for her."

"But if you love someone..." Brooke understood how a newspaper article could reveal secrets and begin a chain of events no one could stop. Her gaze met Nate's, and she knew the feelings she had for him were becoming irrevocable ones.

"Exactly. Apparently, I loved *her* but what she felt for me was in question. And the hardest part of all of it was severing ties with Kristi. I miss the sunshine she brought into my life." Nate shrugged. "So I guess what that says is that Linda wasn't my soul mate, and maybe I wanted the relationship more to be a father than to be a husband.''

They both glanced over at Tessa, who was sleeping soundly now, turned away from them. Angel was curled up at her feet, and Frisco lay by her side.

"I never expected to feel so much," Brooke murmured. "I'm getting really attached to her. And if Dad flies back to France again after he's better—"

"Maybe he'll stay."

"I'd like to believe that. But I can never count on him."

"That could change. Especially if he knows you've made a connection with Tessa."

"Connections have never meant very much to my dad. But he did say that when he married Helena and had Tessa, his view of life changed."

"Then there's hope." Nate was looking down at her as if he wanted to give her hope…maybe a lot more. Could she take the risk of letting him?

Her heart answered for her as he slipped his arm around her and his head bent to hers. The crackle of the fire was the only sound in the room as Nate's lips took hers. His seduction of her mouth was thorough, as he held her masterfully, as his tongue coaxed hers expertly, as the desire that constantly hung between them grew in strength and hunger. She had never known such a deep need, such a heart-wrenching longing to give herself to someone. The sound of the logs disappearing into flame faded into the background. She laced her fingers into Nate's hair, inhaling his male scent…letting herself be drugged by it. His kiss filled her with excitement and hope and a passion so deep-seated it seemed to come from the very essence of who she was.

When his hold loosened a bit, she thought he was going

to break off the kiss. The disappointment that filled her was so great it almost took her breath away. Then she realized Nate didn't just want to kiss her, he wanted to touch her. As his hand slid under her sweater, his fingers were warm and rough. His hand was large and as his thumb made a small circle on her midriff, she thought she'd melt under the caress. His touch was so gentle as he moved his hand up, up, upward and cupped her breast. The intimacy between them seemed right and it made her tremble.

She'd never given herself completely to a man. She'd loved Tim, but she'd hesitated in taking that last intimate step. Maybe because she'd instinctively known he couldn't accept her...everything about her.

Now with Nate, she felt no hesitation. Everything felt so right. If Tessa wasn't sleeping a few feet away—

Nate broke the kiss murmuring close to her ear, "I want you."

"I want you, too," she returned. "But we can't. Tessa..."

"I know," he said with a husky sigh as he tilted his forehead against hers. "And it's not just Tessa. I have to know you'll stay."

It was obvious from Nate's move to Whisper Rock and everything he'd told her, that he wanted a quiet, simple life and a family. She couldn't promise him quiet or simple, and she didn't know what would happen in six months or a year. "I can't promise you that, Nate. I just can't."

His hand lowered from her breast, and as he withdrew his hand she could feel his emotional withdrawal, also.

"I could never understand living in the moment," he said tersely. "The thing is...you don't seem to be that kind of woman."

"What kind of woman?" she asked.

"The kind who believes a night of pleasure is enough."

"I'm *not* that way."

He took her shoulders firmly into both hands. "Then tell me why you can't stay. Tell my why you can't put down roots. Tell me why permanence is such a strange concept to you."

"I can't."

"That won't wash anymore, Brooke. You could tell me. But you *won't*. I know it has something to do with that phone call and something to do with the man in your past."

She heard the hurt in his words. Inside of her a voice was screaming, *If you tell him, he'll send you away. He won't want you to practice here. He'll think you're odd and misguided, if not downright crazy.*

Moving a few inches away from him, she murmured, "I'll bunk on the floor with Tessa. You can have the sofa."

"The hell you will!" he growled. "The sofa opens up into a bed. You and Tessa can take it. I'll sleep on the air mattress."

She knew from the determined look on his face that nothing she said would change his mind. She could give in on this. But she couldn't give in to the desire to find a home in his arms, in his house, in his bed, or in his life.

Chapter Six

Brooke hurried toward her office to check on Tessa. While she was seeing patients, Ellie was keeping her little sister occupied. Fortunately, Tessa liked the motherly woman, and Ellie loved playing with the three-year-old. Her grandchildren lived in Texas, and Ellie didn't see them as often as she'd like. Brooke was glad Nate had fostered this arrangement. But since then, he'd kept his distance.

It had been a week since Nate had kissed her and touched her and told her he wanted her…a week since she'd told him she couldn't promise to stay. They'd slept in his living room that night, mightily aware of each other. In the morning, breakfast had been awkward. Thank goodness the electricity had come back on shortly afterward, and Brooke had taken Tessa and Angel back to their apartment. Except to consult on a case or to discuss Ellie watching Tessa, she and Nate had hardly spoken for days.

Over the weekend she'd taken Tessa to Phoenix to see their father. He'd come home from the hospital, looking pale and frail. When Cal had taken Tessa into his arms, kissed her, hugged her and read her a story, Brooke's heart had twisted. Yet she was glad for Tessa...glad her dad seemed to know how to be a father now. Cal had asked her to keep Tessa for another week until he was truly feeling stronger, and Brooke had agreed. She wasn't ready to break the bonds she was forming with her sister...wasn't ready to let go.

Peeking into her office now, she saw Tessa settled on the air mattress Nate had placed on the floor so she wouldn't be sitting on the cold tile. He was a considerate man. Brooke remembered again how he'd kissed her...the glory of his fingers on her skin...the way he made her dream as she hadn't in a long time.

Tessa's giggle drew Brooke's attention into her office where Ellie was helping her build a Lego tower while Frisco watched. Brooke smiled and opened the door a little wider. Suddenly the bell above the door in the reception area rang, then the door banged shut.

A woman's voice called, "Please! Can someone help me?" as children chattered.

Seeing that Tessa was happily occupied, Brooke hurried to the waiting room.

Dorothy Warner was standing at the reception desk with tears rolling down her cheeks. In her arms she held a rust-and-cream Pomeranian. Jenny stood at her mom's side along with two other girls that looked to be about the same age.

As soon as Dorothy saw Brooke, she rushed to her. "You've got to help Biscuit. She was chasing a raven from the second-story deck and she fell off. I think her leg's broken."

The Pomeranian was whimpering, and Brooke could tell she was in pain. It hurt her terribly to see an animal suffer. Tenderly, she took the dog from Dorothy's arms. When she circled the dog's leg with her fingers, she could feel so much cold she knew the leg *was* broken. As a familiar tingle began in her own fingers, she suspected she could help Biscuit without having to set and cast the leg.

To Dorothy and the girls she said, "Wait here," and hurried to the first open exam room.

Dorothy protested as she followed Brooke, and the children tagged along. "I want to stay with her. I told her I wouldn't leave her."

As Brooke kept walking, she heard the kennel door open and close and glimpsed Nate as he entered the hall. She didn't stop.

In the exam room, instead of placing the dog on the table, she took her to the counter and kept the animal in front of her as her back blocked Dorothy's view. Putting one hand on the dog's spine, she wrapped her other around the broken leg.

Biscuit didn't make a sound.

When Brooke looked into the little dog's eyes, she knew Biscuit understood she was going to help.

Both of Brooke's hands tingled and grew hot as she closed her eyes, letting the energy that was coursing through her flow into Biscuit. She envisioned the bone in Biscuit's leg knitting together...becoming whole... becoming strong. The flow of energy almost vibrated.

The little dog trembled and Brooke bent to murmur, "It's okay, Biscuit. You'll soon be okay."

"What are you doing?" Dorothy asked, coming around the table.

"I'm calming her so I can examine her more easily," Brooke answered.

Heat was still flowing, and she had to wait until it stopped. Her fingers felt as if they sparked with energy she'd never understand but now accepted. Granna had told her long ago that she should always follow her instincts, always look toward the light. Encouraging Brooke, Granna had explained Brooke's great-grandmother had been gifted, too, and Brooke shouldn't be afraid.

It had taken Brooke years not to be afraid…to recognize the tingles, the heat, the warmth and the cold…to distinguish how and where she should use her gift. When she was a child, she'd asked her grandmother so many questions, but Granna had simply explained this gift was from the Master. She had encouraged Brooke to pray for direction every day, asking how best to use it.

All of a sudden the heat and tingling stopped. Biscuit's trembling ceased, and then the little dog stood on her hind legs, licking Brooke's face.

"What happened?" Dorothy Warner asked. "She doesn't seem to be in pain anymore!"

Using her gift was the simple part; explaining what she'd done was another matter entirely. From experience, she knew better than to talk about energy and a healing force that came from inside her…around her…from the mountains and oceans and all of creation.

Brooke lifted Biscuit, setting her on the table. The animal ran over to Dorothy and Jenny, and Dorothy stared at Brooke in amazement.

Now Brooke saw that Nate had come into the room, too. Although he was hanging back, there was an expression on his face that told her she was in trouble.

Maybe not. If she could convince Dorothy…

"The injury wasn't as serious as you thought," Brooke explained. "Her leg was really just locked…sprained a little. I manipulated it. It might still be sore, but if you pamper her for a few days, I'm sure she'll be good as new.''

All smiles now, Dorothy asked, ''You mean it was sort of like me going to a chiropractor?''

Brooke took a relieved breath. ''Yes. Just like that.''

Although Dorothy and the other two children seemed satisfied with the explanation, Jenny was looking at Brooke curiously. And so was Nate.

Knowing the best thing to do was draw the attention from herself, Brooke suggested, ''Let's take her out to the waiting room.''

Once there, Dorothy set Biscuit on the floor, and the dog ran to the door ready to go home.

''She really seems fine. I can't thank you enough. I was sure she was seriously hurt...'' Dorothy took her checkbook from her pocket.

Brooke shook her head and made a dismissive gesture. ''No charge for this. If you'd have put her down on the ground again, she might have worked out the kink herself.''

''You're sure about that?''

''I'm positive. Besides, Jenny brought me Angel. I could never repay you for the happiness she brings me. My little sister loves her, too. So we're more than even.''

Dorothy profusely thanked Brooke again, picked up Biscuit and opened the door.

Jenny was the last to leave. When she looked at Brooke, there was an expression on her face that said her mother might believe in the kink and chiropractor theory, but she didn't.

When the door closed, Brooke turned to face Nate. She could see he didn't believe the theory, either.

''In my office,'' he said tersely.

''I should check on Tessa—''

"Tessa's fine with Ellie. In my office. Now."

After Brooke followed Nate inside, he shut the door. As soon as it clicked shut, he rounded on her. "What happened in there?"

The moment of truth had arrived. Her feelings for Nate went deep, and she wasn't going to lie to him. Choosing her words carefully, she began, "I have a gift, Nate. At least, that's what my Granna calls it."

His eyes narrowed. "What kind of gift?"

"It's not something I can explain," she said honestly. "And I don't really understand it. Granna told me her mother had it, too. It comes from light and the universe, and from the source of whatever gives us life. I'm simply an instrument…a conductor."

A flash of astonishment passed over Nate's face, then his expression became stoic once more, and she couldn't read anything in his eyes but questions.

"Are you telling me that Biscuit's leg was broken and you healed it?" he demanded.

"Yes."

His disbelief was evident as he challenged her. "Why didn't Angel get better as soon as you touched her? Or Mrs. Clark's cat? Or Chad Thompson's Doberman?"

Trying to find the words, Brooke sank against the corner of his desk and remembered this exact scene with Tim, trying to answer the same questions. "I can't heal every animal. At least, not that way. It's as if some are chosen, or I have more of a connection with some than others. And this gift… It's not just for healing."

Nate went still. "What do you mean?"

"Sometimes I can diagnose with it. An owner might bring an animal to me and not know what's wrong. I use my hands and sometimes I can feel cool spots where the problem is. So...even before I do blood tests, X-rays or scans, I know what's wrong.''

''But you do the tests anyway?''

''To confirm what I suspect.''

Now Nate looked worried as he absorbed what she'd told him. Finally he let out a long breath. ''This is why you move from place to place?''

''Not because I want to Nate, but because I have to. I went to school at the University of Illinois because I won a full scholarship there. After I graduated, I couldn't afford to start a practice of my own, so I sent out résumés. I wanted to move closer to Granna again, but I had to make a living. So I joined a practice in a suburb of Chicago.'' She stopped, not knowing how much she should tell him.

''Go on,'' he commanded, crossing his arms, looking like a judge assessing evidence.

''I'd been there a year when I met Tim Peabody,'' she said in a low voice. ''I thought we'd have a future together. But then someone brought in a parakeet who'd been chased by a dog and was badly hurt. For whatever reason, I was able to heal that bird, and another vet and an assistant saw it. Word spread. I refused an interview with a reporter who called, and he wrote an article, anyway. Tim was...upset to say the least. He wanted to make partner in his law firm and he didn't want his colleagues to think he was involved with a kook. I began getting crank calls, and everyone at the clinic looked at me as if I belonged in outer space. Then Tim decided I was a liability and broke off our relationship. I left and ended up in Syracuse.''

Silent moments ticked by until Nate asked, ''What happened in Syracuse?''

She could feel Nate pulling back, withdrawing further away from her. "Nate…"

"What happened in Syracuse?" he repeated.

"The same thing that happened here. I put my hands on an animal…" She trailed off. "Just like today, in Syracuse no one was sure exactly what happened with a cat who had been in kidney failure but whose next set of tests came back all right. I can go for months practicing like a normal vet, and then suddenly there's that animal that I'm supposed to help. It doesn't matter who's around me or what they see, I have to follow my instincts and my intuition. I can't let an animal suffer, no matter what helping them means to my life."

Nate drove his hand through his hair. "I see now why you didn't want to tell me anything about this. It's unbelievable."

"I know." She also knew she was looking to him for acceptance, for openness to what she'd told him, for a chance to stay and make her life work. But his expression could have been carved on a mountain. The way he looked at her now was different from the way he'd looked at her before.

"Do you want me to leave?" she asked, squaring her shoulders, preparing for the inevitable.

"I need to think about all of it, Brooke. What I saw with Biscuit isn't easy to accept. What you've told me isn't easy to accept. I have my practice to think about, and the clinic's reputation."

She knew that all too well. "Do you want me to continue to work here while you think about it?"

Pacing across the office, he asked, "How much longer will you be taking care of Tessa?"

"Until the weekend. I'll keep working the morning

hours with you if Ellie can watch her. Saturday I'll take her home. I'll be back Sunday afternoon.''

He stopped pacing and faced her. ''I'll have an answer for you then.''

His tone was as serious as Brooke had ever heard it. ''I wish I could have told you about all of this from the beginning.''

As his gaze passed over her face, there was turmoil in his eyes that matched hers. ''I think you wish you didn't have to tell me at all. Let's get back to work,'' he said curtly, as he left his office.

Brooke's heart was heavy with the possibility that Nate Stanton would put his practice and the stability of his life ahead of any feelings he had for her.

What else could she expect?

After dinner at Granna's on Saturday evening, Cal Pennington asked Brooke, ''Take a walk with me?''

''Me, too?'' Tessa asked from Brooke's elbow with an expectant smile.

''How about you stay here and keep Granna company?'' Cal suggested. ''We won't be long. When we come in, you can tell me more about this dog who catches snowballs in his mouth.''

That seemed to satisfy Tessa as she went back to shoveling in a bite of the cherry pie Granna had made.

Brooke was a bit anxious as she and Cal walked from the house to the barn. The temperature was much warmer than a few hours north in Whisper Rock. The scent of citrus rode on the night air, and she concentrated on that, not knowing what to expect from her father.

Uncomfortable with the silence, she broke it. ''You're looking better,'' she said, because he was. Despite the incision on his neck and bruising around it, there was color in his face now, and he seemed to have more energy.

"I'm feeling better, too. The Doc said it will be another week or two until I'm really back up to snuff."

Probably her dad would be gone after those weeks. Maybe she'd get the opportunity to spend more time with Tessa before that happened.

"Tessa's going to miss being with you," he said. "I can tell."

"I'm going to miss *her*."

Cal stopped walking and looked Brooke over. "You're nothing like your mother. You know that?"

"No, I don't know that. I've wondered. I mean, I know I don't look like her. I've seen pictures. She was blond—"

"I don't mean looks," he said, shaking his head. "I mean who you are down deep inside. You took to Tessa like she was born to you."

"She's my sister." The *half* had slipped away during the days Brooke had spent with Tessa.

He was silent for a few moments, then started walking again. "I was afraid you'd be like Gail. I was afraid you might not want Tessa around. But Granna said it wouldn't be like that, and she was right."

"Granna's usually right."

"Yes, she is. And I'm usually wrong. I never should have stayed with your mother. Or run off with her and left you. I should have realized she was just a selfish woman who didn't want any responsibility laid on her. But she was beautiful, Brooke. Such a free spirit. She was ready for any adventure I could cook up. She looked at me like I was her world, and I couldn't resist that."

Brooke wanted to see that look in a man's eyes for her.

Still… "What about after my mother died? You could have taken me then."

"I was twenty-one. I didn't have a stable job. After your mother died, I didn't even want one. For a couple of years I drank, out of regret and guilt for leaving you behind. Mom sent me money when she probably shouldn't have, and it kept me going. Then I began back-packing through Europe. The farther I traveled, the less I drank. But I knew I couldn't take care of you like she could. And I was just too damn selfish to come back here, get some nine-to-five job and be responsible. I'm sorry for that, and yet I also know that being with me wouldn't have been good for you."

She'd blamed herself all these years for her dad not staying. If she had been cuter…smarter… "Why is it different with Tessa?" She had to know.

"When I met Helena, I'd had enough of traveling. I had gotten a job that I liked at a vineyard. I not only learned about making wine, but about managing a facility that size. Helena owned a small bakery in town. When we married, we lived in a cottage on the vineyard, and I'd never been happier. Then Tessa came along, and she was a bonus. Helena was a wonderful mother, Brooke. Kind, and tender and doting…like you are with Tessa." His voice became husky. "I'll never stop missing her."

Tears pricked Brooke's eyes as she realized her father wasn't the uncaring, callous man she had always thought he was. His aloofness when he'd visited her wasn't from lack of caring, but had stemmed from regret, guilt and simply not knowing how to be with a child. Understanding that helped somehow.

"Are you going to go back to the vineyard?" The life he'd made with Helena was there, and it might be too precious to leave behind.

"I don't know yet. Since surgery, I've just tried to concentrate on getting stronger and not much else. I didn't want Mom to have the burden of caring for Tessa and me, too."

"She wouldn't consider caring for Tessa a burden."

"I know that. I'm grateful you didn't, either."

"I didn't know how I'd feel about Tessa," she responded truthfully. "At first when I learned about her, I resented her because she was the child you loved—the child you kept with you."

"Brooke—" Her name was strangled in his throat.

She held up her hand to stop him. "But then you asked me to take care of her and every minute she was with me, I wanted to protect her…love her. That first night I took her home, I think she was afraid in a strange place and she asked me not to leave her. I told her I wouldn't. I want to always be there if she needs me."

They'd arrived at the corral fence, and now Cal crossed his arms over the top rung and looked out into the night. "I abandoned you, Brooke. I know every bit of what that means. I know you should be bitter and resentful and hate me."

"I don't hate you," she murmured.

"I guess that's a start. But whether I stay around here or not, the question I need answered is—can you ever forgive me?"

When Brooke returned from Phoenix she went up to her apartment…and missed Tessa.

"Hi, Angel," she said to the small kitten who came to greet her. "It's just you and me again. It might be you and me somewhere else soon."

Can you ever forgive me? Her father's words haunted her because she hadn't been able to give him an answer.

Her feelings about her father were as upside down as her relationship with Nate. Relationship. She didn't even know if she had a relationship anymore. Or if she ever had. Maybe it had all been in her mind. Desire was a far cry from deep feelings. Nate had wanted her to promise to stay. She hadn't been able to. Now he probably wanted her to go. The only person in her life who had ever loved her unconditionally, who had stayed firm and in the same spot, so she would always be there to come back to, was Granna. Yet in a way she knew if she wanted to be a self-sufficient woman, Granna belonged to her childhood. Brooke didn't know what she wanted more—bonds or answers to all the unresolved questions in her life.

Brooke's fingers stroked through Angel's fur, giving pleasure to the animal and comfort to herself. When the kitten licked her finger, Brooke picked her up and held her against her cheek. "It's going to be you and me, kiddo. I promise wherever I go, I'll take you with me. Are you hungry?"

As if she understood, the kitten gave a little "meow." Such simple communication brought a smile to Brooke's face. Animals were so much easier to deal with than people.

When she looked out her window, she saw no movement over at Nate's house. Frisco wasn't in the yard. Nate was going to give her his decision today, and she couldn't just sit and anxiously wait for it.

Seeing her skis propped in the corner she knew what she was going to do. She needed exercise, fresh air and open space to calm her, to ready her for whatever she had to do next.

Brooke took her ski suit, bright yellow with turquoise bands around the elbows and knees, from the back of her closet. After she mixed vitamins with the cat food for

Angel, she dressed quickly, gave the kitten a last tender caress and went down the stairs. There was still no sign of Nate, and she wondered what he did on his days off…who he spent them with. He was on call this weekend for the vet in Flagstaff, and he might have had to make a trip there for an emergency.

The anxiety over whether she would be staying or leaving, over how Nate's opinion of her had changed, over the uncertainty of everything in her life right now, hit her hard as she adjusted her sunglasses and with purpose pushed off across the fields. Even when she'd lived in Syracuse, she'd managed to get out of the city now and then to cross-country ski at the closest resort.

Out here, she loved the wind on her face, the sun shimmering on the snow, the scenery of tall pines, cottonwoods, split-rail fences. It seemed as if she could see forever.

Yet…she was probably skiing today because she was looking for tomorrow.

The silence of boundless country was always her friend. Sometimes she found answers in it. As she pushed herself harder and faster with her poles over fresh snow that had fallen yesterday morning, the sun dimmed in the blue sky and clouds swept over it. Brooke paid the weather no mind. The rhythm of cross-country skiing took over and she seemed to sail across the fields, unmindful of the time, as every once in a while she took her compass from her pocket and kept heading due north. She could follow her ski tracks back, but if for some reason she lost them, she would only have to head south.

A short time later she reached a band of pines and saw there was a trail through them, rutted with tracks from snowmobiles.

Five minutes later she emerged from the trees. The sky

was gray, and she knew the early dusk could mean the weather was changing. But she needed this release. She needed this grounding with the earth, the trees, the sky and something much greater than she was. Maybe then she could make the decisions that mattered, whether she stayed in Whisper Rock or not.

When she reached the base of a ridge, she realized where she was—Whisper Rock. Nate had described the unusual rock formation that sprang from the ridge overlooking the surrounding area. Suddenly it was important to reach it, to listen and to hope it would whisper answers to her.

Heedless of the gray sky, Brooke made a sideways climb to the crest. There she could look down over the landscape. She'd been climbing during her whole excursion and realized the return trip would be much easier. As she gazed north and east, she knew she was looking at reservation land—Hopi and Navajo. There were mesas and plateaus. To the west she glimpsed a house with a barn in the distance backed by rolling hills and Ponderosa pine forests. Split-rail fence divided the landscape. To the south, the pines gave way to cottonwood and scrub.

The beauty of it all overwhelmed her, and as she stood at the base of Whisper Rock, tears came to her eyes when she thought about leaving. She wasn't sure she'd ever felt so strongly about a place before...or about a man. When Tim had cut off their relationship and she'd left, she'd missed him. But she hadn't felt as if she'd left a piece of her behind.

As she stared at the sky and waited, Whisper Rock was silent. Her eyes closed, and she felt something wet on her face. Looking up, she saw flurries of snow come wafting down. It was time to head back...to Nate and his decision.

After she descended the hill, she started off toward the trees, her skis picking up speed on the downhill slope.

The treeline was about thirty yards ahead. She was thinking about Nate and his reaction to what had happened to Biscuit—the withdrawal in his eyes, his whole demeanor becoming guarded. She couldn't expect him to understand. She couldn't expect him to accept something that had taken her years to accept herself. Her eyes blurred with unshed tears and she barely saw the uneven ground before her. Not having time to slow, she hit a mound of brush and snow. Instead of sailing over it, her ski twisted sideways. Thrown off balance, she fell and her poles flew. When she landed, the breath was knocked out of her. Although her left boot had detached from her ski, the right one hadn't. She felt the wrenching pain of the twist and heard an echo of her voice as she cried out.

Stunned, she just lay there for a moment. Then she sat up, the pain throbbing so hard she had to take a few deep breaths. This kind of thing had never happened before....

Today her mind had been so full of Nate and the decisions she had to make that she'd been careless. Shaking her head at her stupidity, she tried to get up. The pain in her right ankle kept her from putting weight on the foot. Skiing back was out of the question. Taking off her right ski, she used it to help herself up. She was in the middle of nowhere. It was up to her to get back. She'd either have to crawl or hop. Those were her options.

Don't feel sorry for yourself, Brooke, a voice in her head whispered. *Just get going.*

Using her skis as makeshift crutches, Brooke started toward the veterinary clinic, hoping she had enough grit to make it before her ankle or her spirit gave out altogether.

Chapter Seven

When Nate turned his SUV into the clinic's parking lot late Sunday afternoon, he saw Brooke's van and his heart beat faster. He was glad she was back. More than glad, he had to admit, as the thought of her heated his blood. Yet when he thought about seeing her again, reality clubbed him.

Veering toward his driveway, he said to Frisco, who was sitting on the passenger seat, "I don't know what the hell to do about her. It's damn near impossible to believe what I saw, almost as impossible to believe what she said. And even if it's all true..."

He pushed the button on the garage door's remote. "What will it mean to the clinic? Everyone will call her a crackpot. And if people do believe she can do what she says she can do, we'll draw terminally ill animals here from the West Coast to the East Coast, publicity about it, maybe even news coverage."

Pulling into the garage, he didn't shut the door. He'd

take Frisco for a walk first—a short walk from the looks of the weather.

Frisco could definitely romp faster in the snow than Nate could tramp. Instead of heading for the stand of cottonwoods behind the clinic, though, Frisco veered north, sniffing.

As Nate followed the dog, he saw the tracks in the snow.

Frisco barked at him, ran a few feet ahead and then barked again.

Nate remembered the skis he'd carried up to Brooke's apartment. Would she have taken off this late in the day with the weather turning? It was easy to see the tracks began to the rear of the clinic. They had to be hers. As he searched the area for a return set of tracks, he found none.

"Come on, boy. Let's make sure these are Brooke's. If they are—then I think you're going to wait in the house while I take out the snowmobile."

A few minutes later, as snow fell heavier and he grew more worried, Nate took his machine from its shed in the backyard and ran it at full throttle. He couldn't imagine Brooke being out in this. From the way she talked, she wasn't a beginner at cross-country skiing. What had pushed her to set out today? Something that had happened in Phoenix? His reaction to what she'd done for Biscuit?

He remembered the look in her eyes that had pleaded with him to believe her, to stick by her. Yet everything that had happened to him in L.A. made him leery of notoriety. He just wanted to live his life without the world looking in.

Nate revved up the snowmobile and took it to its capacity as the snow came down harder. When he reached the grove of pines, he had to slow. Under the canopy and in the shelter of the trees, it was almost dark. He switched on his headlights and was proceeding semicautiously when he saw movement. An animal? Brooke?

His heart almost stopped. His gut clenched. Then he spotted the upraised arm and knew it *was* Brooke. She was leaning on her ski. "Are you all right?" he shouted, then hurried to her.

Closer now, in the glow of the headlights, he could see her face. She looked embarrassed. "Just feeling stupid," she said loud enough for him to hear her over the snowmobile engine. She pointed to her boot. "I twisted my ankle. It probably would have taken me all night to hobble back."

"And you would have done just that, too, wouldn't you?" he muttered, standing close to her, needing to make sure she was okay.

"How did you know to come searching?" she asked.

"Some of that intuition you value so highly," he said, still not knowing if he believed in any of it. As he spoke into her ear, the brush of her skin against his lips thoroughly aroused him.

Pride squared her shoulders as she stepped back. "I didn't ask you to come looking for me. I didn't ask you to get me out of this. You can just turn around and go back right now if you're going to have a superior attitude about it. I've had enough of—"

Her voice broke, her chin quivered, and Nate felt like the biggest heel on the face of the planet.

Without giving her any warning, he swung her up into his arms.

As her skis fell to the ground, she gasped, "What are you doing?"

"Putting you in the snowmobile and taking you back before we can't find our way. I'll collect your skis and poles tomorrow.'' He felt her gaze on him, but he didn't look at her because he didn't have answers for her...yet. ''Do you think the ankle is broken?'' he asked as he settled her on the back of the bench.

''I'm hoping it's just a sprain.''

''We'll find out soon enough,'' he said. ''I'll take you to the emergency room.''

''All it needs is some ice...''

''You can't be going up and down those stairs if you've done serious damage.''

That caused Brooke to be silent. He climbed onto the bench in front of her and they headed back.

Darkness had fallen by the time Nate transferred Brooke from his snowmobile to his SUV. Once belted inside, she said, ''I need a favor.''

''Angel,'' he responded without her even having to say it.

Brooke nodded. ''She needs food and medicine. We might be at the hospital a while....''

''I'll be back in ten minutes. And I'll remember to talk to her and pet her, too.''

''Thanks.'' Brooke's smile was wobbly, and it made his chest ache for what they could have. Yet he also knew she would leave again eventually.

''No thanks necessary.'' He told himself he'd do as much for anyone.

Fortunately, when they arrived at the hospital in Flagstaff a half hour later, the emergency room wasn't busy. Brooke insisted on walking to the waiting area, and he could tell she was in a lot of pain. After she filled out the required paperwork, a nurse called her back to a cubicle and Nate went with her. He offered her his arm, and she leaned heavily on him as she walked...slowly.

They were waiting for the doctor in a sterile little room

when Nate asked her, "Do you want me to try to take your boot off? It's going to hurt. The doctor might be able to do a better job of it."

"You do it." She looked up at him with eyes that said she trusted him not to hurt her more than necessary.

After he unlaced her boot, he pulled the tongue as far forward as he could, stretching the leather all the way around. Probing her ankle with gentle fingers, he muttered, "It's swollen."

"I thought the cold might keep the swelling down."

"It did some. But this is still going to hurt. Ready?"

She nodded.

He tried to ease the boot off, but she pressed her lips together firmly against the pain. His chest tightened. He didn't want to hurt Brooke. Not in any way.

After he set the boot on the floor, she breathed a sigh of relief and opened her eyes. With her foot in his hand, he undid the zipper at the ankle of her ski pants, then rolled down her sock. Her foot seemed so fragile and delicate, though he knew Brooke wasn't fragile *or* delicate.

"I have to ask you something," he said gruffly.

She unzipped her ski jacket. "What?"

"Why can't you heal your ankle like you healed Biscuit?" Crouched in front of her, he saw the play of emotions on her face.

Snatching off her hat, she held it tightly in her hands. "I can only heal animals, Nate, not humans. Granna told me that's not unusual. It was the same with her mother."

In spite of himself he was curious. "When did it start? I mean, I've heard of people having special abilities after they're hit by lightning..."

She shook her head. "It wasn't like that. This gift has sort of...grown...as I did...as I learned to use it."

"When was the first time?"

"I think I always had a special affinity for animals. They were always around the ranch. We had horses and a few cattle, cats and kittens constantly playing around the barn. The very first time it happened—"

She stopped for a moment and studied him carefully. Then, as if she'd decided not to hold anything back, she went on. "One of my favorite kittens disappeared overnight. I went looking for her. I found Calico in a neighbor's field by a fencepost, and she was hardly breathing. When I held her in my hands, I had this unusual feeling in my fingers. Sort of like heat mixed with tingling and then cold. When I put her down it stopped. She was so little and I loved her a lot."

Brooke's voice caught, and she cleared her throat. "When I picked her up again, the tingling, the heat and the cold all started up once more. I began petting her, and as I did, I felt hot and cold spots in places that seemed to be asking for my touch. I took her back to the barn and I sat with her in the stall all day, holding her, touching one place, then moving on to another when it seemed right. By that evening I'd managed to feed her a little milk with an eye dropper. Before I went to bed, she ate some solid food for me and was standing up. I could tell she was stronger. I could see something had changed. I didn't know enough to be afraid of what I'd done. But I didn't tell anybody about it, either, not even Granna. On some level I knew something extraordinary had happened."

Straightening, fascinated by everything Brooke was telling him, he sat in the chair beside the gurney. "When did it happen again?"

This time she didn't hesitate. "I was at the neighbor's. I often went over there to ride Mr. Swenson's pony. One of his horses had colic. Granna had come over to pick me up, and Mr. Swenson went to get medicine for the horse. I put my hands on the horse's belly. By the time Mr. Swenson got back to the barn, I'd led Marlboro outside and he was fine. I told Mr. Swenson the horse had just walked it off. But Granna knew better. On the way home she told me about her own mother. She said I should explore everything about my gift and use it wisely whenever I could.''

''No one else knew?''

''No. No one else knew. In high school I asked Granna all kinds of questions that she couldn't answer—about where the gift came from and what it meant. I think I just wanted to believe it wasn't so strange after all. I told my best friend about it. But the look in her eyes when I did...'' Brooke's eyes glistened as she thought about it. Pushing her hair behind her ear, she went on. ''Donna must have thought I was lying or else very strange. She wasn't my friend after that. She kept her distance. When I told Granna what had happened, she told me to pray every day and keep myself as close to good as I could. I understand what she meant now, but back then it was all such a puzzle.''

Nate thought about everything she said...a little girl dealing with so much.

For a few moments Brooke's gaze locked to his. ''It just seemed obvious I should become a veterinarian. I couldn't heal every hurt animal. The surges of energy were sporadic, and I could never predict when they would occur. Now I just try to follow the flow of energy and the sensations, using my intuition. I know in my heart and soul it's what I'm supposed to do.''

The thought of all Brooke had gone through, and the extraordinary gift he was beginning to face, was hard to absorb. "So when other people are around, you try to cover it up?"

"It seems best. Most people don't understand animals very well, so it's not difficult to do."

He turned to stare at the counter with its medical paraphernalia as if he was seeing exactly what had taken place. "I don't think Dorothy Warner realized exactly what happened."

"No, I don't think she did. But eventually, somebody does notice, Nate. I know you have to take that into consideration."

As his gaze focused on Brooke once more, he realized she was making him sound like a judge. Maybe she felt he was. He didn't like that role. He didn't like it at all. He was simply concerned about his practice and his patients and keeping his business alive. And yet Brooke concerned him, too. He didn't want her to leave.

No matter what her staying brings you? his logical voice asked him.

"I want you to stay, Brooke. I can't offer you the partnership under these circumstances, but I do want you to stay."

She was very still for a moment. "Thank you," she said with gratitude he didn't want. "I'll do everything I can to try to keep things 'normal.' Besides, nothing unusual might happen again for a year. That's the way it works."

The longing to take Brooke's hands in his was so strong he clenched his hands into fists. He wanted to kiss her again and take her into his arms and tell her everything was going to be okay. But he didn't know if it would be okay. If she couldn't keep this gift of hers under wraps, all hell would break loose. He didn't want to be involved in it. He didn't want to get wrapped up in Brooke, knowing she might be leaving any day. So he'd have to keep his distance. That was the safest way to handle all of it.

A young doctor with a friendly smile pushed open the curtain, and Nate was glad. He and Brooke shouldn't spend time alone...not if he wanted to keep their relationship platonic. It would be difficult but not impossible. He assured himself platonic would be the best for both of them.

After Nate finished his yearly exam of Mrs. Morrison's poodle late Wednesday morning, he decided to get another cup of coffee before seeing his next patient. He went out to the desk, caught sight of Brooke standing by the magazine rack with Craig Torrence and frowned. They both seemed intently involved in their discussion. Nate noticed how close Craig was standing to Brooke and felt more annoyance when the accountant smiled at Brooke as if she were the only woman on earth.

Brooke wasn't using her crutches today, and earlier Nate had noticed she'd only limped slightly. After the X-rays, the doctor had told her she'd sprained her ankle and needed to be on crutches for a few days to give it a rest, along with elevating it and icing it whenever she could. But she hadn't let it slow her down. She'd insisted on a full roster of patients both Monday and Tuesday. She was stubborn, that was for sure. He'd invited her to stay at his house so she wouldn't have to climb the stairs. She'd refused, and he'd known why. They were like dynamite—hot, explosive, ready to go up in flames—whenever they were alone together for too long.

Brooke was wary of him because she was afraid he couldn't accept her gift, afraid he'd ask her to leave at the first sign of trouble. He was wary of her because he wasn't sure of what he thought of all of it, or where she fit into his life.

Craig Torrence gave Brooke's elbow a squeeze, and Nate moved toward them without thinking twice. Torrence was divorced and had a reputation for dating any single woman who showed interest. Nate didn't like Torrence looking at Brooke as if she were the next affair on his list.

"Hi, Craig," Nate said with more friendliness than he felt. He nodded to the carrier on the bench where Torrence's huge, yellow tabby sat. "How's Delilah? You just had her in for shots last month. Is something wrong?"

Craig was sandy-haired with blue eyes that could charm and seduce. He wasn't as tall as Nate, but he was fit, and Nate had to admit the ladies seemed to like him. Now he handled Nate's question with the nonchalance Nate wished he felt. "Delilah needed her claws trimmed. You know how I hate to do it. Fortunately, it gave me a chance to meet your new associate."

Smiling at them both, Brooke said easily, "I was telling Craig about a natural sisal scratching post that has catnip embedded in it. Delilah might like it better than his new recliner."

"I'm going to send for one," Torrence assured her. "But in the meantime..." He took a look at Nate that said he wished Nate would go away. But Nate wasn't going anywhere.

"In the meantime," he repeated, "I asked Brooke if she'd like to go to a movie with me on Sunday."

Both men's attention turned to Brooke.

Her cheeks grew rosy, but she didn't seem flustered. Nate imagined men asked her out all the time.

She smiled at Torrence. "That sounds lovely, Craig. But I have other plans on Sunday. I'm sorry."

"What about Saturday night?" Torrence asked hopefully.

"She joined the crew that's going to work on repairs at Mrs. Barlow's place," Nate revealed with satisfaction, knowing Brooke's plans because he'd signed on with the crew, too.

"Mrs. Barlow's house sure needs help," Torrence was quick to reply. "Those windows are broken in her attic, and the back porch looks like it's going to fall off. Maybe I'll sign on, too, and see you there."

When a friend of Nate's had stopped at the clinic to tell him the chamber of commerce's fix-up group was going to help Mrs. Barlow next, Brooke had overheard and said she'd volunteer, too. Nate had been glad she was getting involved with the community, and yet he knew if she did, it would make it harder for her to leave.

"I signed up for kitchen duty," Brooke informed Torrence.

The man grinned. "I probably won't see much of you then. But I'll save you a seat and maybe we can chat more while we're eating pizzas after we've finished." Before Brooke could refuse him, he smiled at her again. "I'll look forward to seeing you then. I've gotta go now. I have clients coming after lunch. Tax season, you know. Thanks for the tips on Delilah."

After Torrence picked up his cat, he gave Brooke another long smoldering look and exited the clinic.

Nate waited until the door had closed. "If you encourage him, he'll have you in bed on the first date," Nate grumbled.

Brooke's eyes shone with pure amusement. "So he's a fast worker?"

"The fastest. You aren't interested, are you?" He couldn't believe he let that question loose.

"I don't know, Nate. If I'm going to stay, I guess I need to have a social life."

He couldn't tell if she was kidding or not. Then he remembered she'd said she had plans on Sunday. "Are you starting that social life on Sunday?"

"Granna and my father and Tessa are coming to visit. That's not quite the same thing as going out on the town."

Unsettled, Nate felt as if he'd stumbled into a mud bog and didn't know how to get out of it. They gazed at each other for a few moments, and he was so tempted to ask her to go out on the town with him. Yet if he did, they'd end up in bed. He was sure of it. He couldn't be near Brooke and not want a hell of a lot more than friendship. Wanting Brooke, having Brooke, would be only temporary. He'd built his house to have roots and stability, and he wanted a woman who could fit into that. Brooke didn't.

For a moment he thought she looked disappointed he hadn't pursued the idea. But she was standing tall, her face a polite mask. "It'll be nice to see Craig again on Saturday. Maybe I'll ask him to show me around the area. I haven't seen much of it yet."

Her message was clear. If Nate wasn't interested, another man was. And she intended to have a social life. The idea made him more than annoyed this time. It made him downright angry. He didn't like the notion of her being with anyone but him. "You do that," he growled. "But if you do, be prepared for advances that go beyond friendly."

"Don Juans are usually sheep in wolves' clothing. Not the other way around. I can take care of myself, Nate. I have for a very long time."

Although he knew that was true, he also knew there was an innocence about Brooke that he could sense, feel and almost touch. "This Tim you were involved with. Were you lovers?"

He'd never seen Brooke angry, but now he recognized the sparks of it in her eyes. "That's none of your business, Nate."

"No, I guess it's not. Nothing about you is my business, except for the work you do here. I'll try to remember that." Then he turned and walked away from Brooke, toward the reception desk and another mug of coffee.

Picking up the next file in his basket, he asked Ellie sharply, "Which exam room?"

His receptionist eyed him curiously. She hadn't overheard his conversation with Brooke—they'd been too far away for that. But he'd caught her watching them with interest.

"Room three," she answered with a cock of her brow and a tilt of her head. She leaned across the desk and lowered her voice. "You know, Nate, if you're interested in Brooke, you might want to stake a claim. Mr. Donaldson was taken with her, too. He said to me she's a real looker with a brain."

Pete Donaldson was another of Whisper Rock's bachelors. He owned the hardware store. When he'd hit thirty-five last year, Pete had announced he was openly looking for a wife. "It doesn't matter to me what Pete Donaldson thinks," Nate snapped. "Just stay out of this, Ellie. Brooke's her own woman. She does what she wants, and so do I."

Ellie looked hurt at his rebuff. Leaning away from him she said coolly, "Whatever you say, Nate," and sat down at the computer.

"Hell," he muttered under his breath and headed for exam room three. At the rate he was going, nobody would be speaking to him by lunchtime...except Frisco.

* * *

On Sunday Brooke stood in front of the clinic as Granna drove the old green Taurus station wagon into the parking lot. She was so glad to see her family. Nate's aloofness and the cautious way he looked at her upset her greatly. She told herself it was because he was her employer, and he could terminate her at any time. But she knew that wasn't true. She missed the camaraderie they'd shared. She missed that feeling of growing closer to someone who could make a difference in her life. She missed his kisses that had led her to believe desire was only the least of what simmered between them.

Brooke waved at her family and Tessa waved enthusiastically from her car seat in the back. After Granna parked, Cal let Tessa out of her seat.

Her sister came running to her.

Opening her arms wide, Brooke stooped down and caught her. The hug was long as Brooke murmured, "I missed you."

"I miss you, too," Tessa returned. "I wanna play ball wif F'isco and Nate."

During Tessa's stay with Brooke, they'd played ball with Frisco many times, and once Nate joined in. Brooke didn't think Nate would want to see her today. Yesterday, after the men had made repairs on Mrs. Barlow's house and the women had cleaned thoroughly, Brooke had spent a while talking to Craig. They'd sat together eating pizza. He was well traveled, liked animals and had been educated at Stanford. But he wasn't Nate. He said he'd call her soon, but if he did, she knew she'd decline his invitation. She doubted if Craig wanted a platonic friendship, and that's all she could give him.

"I think Nate's busy today," she told Tessa. "How about if you and I show Granna and Dad the clinic? We even have two dogs and a cat in the kennel this weekend. They're staying here while their owners are away.'' She'd just played with them and fed them.

But Tessa shook her head. "Ball. Wif F'isco and Nate.''

Cal came up behind his youngest daughter. "She can be stubborn sometimes.''

Granna gave Brooke a hug and a kiss and said to Tessa, "I'd really like to see where Brooke works. And you know all about it. Can you show me?'' Granna gave Brooke a wink.

"Okay,'' Tessa said, as if it wasn't the first thing she wanted to do. But then she took Granna's hand and pulled her toward the kennels. "See doggies.''

As they disappeared down the hall, Cal stepped beside Brooke. "I think she's going to follow in your footsteps.''

"Children like animals.''

That awkward silence overtook them again. "You're looking good, Dad,'' she said.

"I'm feeling better every day.'' As he unzipped his down parka, Brooke asked, "Would you like a tour, too?''

"I would. But first—'' he shifted from one foot to the other and jabbed his hands into his jeans pockets "—I'd like to ask you something.''

"What?''

"What would you say if I told you I was going to stay in Phoenix?''

Her breath came faster. "*Are* you going to stay in Phoenix?

"That depends.''

"On what?

His brown eyes held hers. "You. I'd like for us to get to know each other better. I'd like you and Tessa to stay close.''

"Dad…"

"I know. Who am I to make demands now after leaving you alone for so many years? But—"

"I don't know if I'm going to stay here. I don't know where I'll go next."

"Why wouldn't you stay here?"

Her father knew nothing about her. Certainly not what had made her move, first from Chicago and then from Syracuse. He might think she was just a roamer as he was. "Maybe I'm like you. Maybe I want to travel. See the country. See the world."

Cal's eyes narrowed as he studied her. "I don't think so. I was searching for something, Brooke. Searching for something I could never find. Or maybe I didn't want to really know where I could find it. I thought living meant excitement and new places and new experiences, and I guess it does to some extent. But now I want peace and some measure of contentment, and I won't find that in France. I think I'll only find that here—with Granna and you and Tessa."

Before she could help herself, she responded, "But you didn't care about me for all these years. Why now?"

He took a deep breath. "It isn't just one thing, Brooke. It's been building for a long time. When Helena died and I faced the full care of Tessa, it was history repeating itself. But this time the world looked different to me. *I* was different. I *wanted* to be responsible for her. I *wanted* to read her bedtime stories. I *wanted* to see everything new she did each day."

The old hurt welled up, and Brooke's eyes filled with tears.

Taking her by the shoulders, he confessed, "I know you should throw me out of your life for good for what I did to you, and for everything I didn't do for you. But

I want to change that. I know I can't make up for not being around when you were growing up. But I can make sure you and Tessa see each other. I can make sure that if you need me now, I'll be here.''

She shook her head. ''It's not so simple. Yes, I'd like to spend time with Tessa. But as far as depending on you—''

''I know you can't now. But in time I'll show you you can. The big question is—do you want me to stay in Phoenix so we can try?''

As she looked into her father's eyes, she tried to see so many things. If she was looking for answers from him, she didn't know if he could give her more than he already had. Could she wipe the slate clean? Could she put aside all those years that she'd hurt because he wasn't there?

She wanted to try. Oh, how she wanted to try. ''I want you to stay in Phoenix.''

Cal didn't get a chance to respond as Tessa and Granna came back from their tour.

Granna glanced from Brooke to Cal. ''Everything okay here?''

''Everything's okay,'' Cal said in a low voice.

Taking Brooke's hand, Tessa pulled her toward the door. ''Nate. F'isco. I wanna play ball.''

Knowing her sister wouldn't be diverted with any more distracting tactics, Brooke faced the inevitable. ''All right. We'll go see if Nate and Frisco are home. But they might not be. And if they are, they might not feel like playing ball.''

Tessa didn't want to hear any of that as she tugged Brooke toward the door.

Chapter Eight

After taking a deep breath, Brooke lifted Tessa to Nate's doorbell. Her sister pressed the button, and Brooke's pulse raced as she lowered her to the ground.

A few moments later Nate came to the door. When he looked at Brooke, his eyes were cold. But then he gave his attention to Tessa, smiled and asked, "What have we here?"

Frisco shoved his nose between Nate's leg and the doorjamb.

Tessa giggled, patted Frisco's head and grinned up at Nate. "Play ball. Wif you and F'isco."

"I told her you might be busy," Brooke said softly, "but she can be very determined when she wants to do something."

Nate's gaze met hers, but it was unreadable. "I'm not busy. I was watching basketball and reading the newspaper. Playing ball would be much better for me than sitting on the couch."

Glancing into the parking lot, he saw Granna's station

wagon. "Are your grandmother and father in your apartment?" he asked.

Even if he was frustrated with her, he seemed to genuinely care about her family. "They're waiting for us in the clinic. If you weren't here, we were going to take a drive into Flagstaff."

"They can wait in here if they'd like. I have a fire going."

With each day that went by, she became more indebted to Nate's kindness. "They won't want to impose."

"It's not an imposition, Brooke," he said with an edge to his voice. "I think they'll be more comfortable in my living room than hiking up the stairs to your apartment and sitting on that lumpy couch."

Brooke thought about it. "All right. I'll tell them."

As Tessa knelt on the porch to pet Frisco, Brooke sneaked a sideways glance at Nate. She was glad they'd be playing ball and not doing something in close quarters. His removed attitude caused an ache that she knew wasn't going to go away. She wanted what they'd had before she'd healed Biscuit. Her gift had caused her problems before, and she'd rearranged her life because of it. But it had never seemed like the burden it was now—a burden that interfered with the friendship and intimacy she'd begun to find with Nate.

He was wearing a red flannel shirt, well-worn jeans and had never looked sexier as he said, "I'll get my jacket and Frisco's ball. You invite your grandmother and father to warm up in front of the fire."

Brooke's heart ached as Nate and Frisco disappeared into the house.

A half hour later while Tessa threw the ball to Nate in his front yard, Brooke glanced up and saw her grandmother standing at the living room window watching them. She was holding the mug of tea Nate had made for her, and Brooke knew her dad was probably sitting in front of the TV watching the basketball game. He was definitely on the mend. His exercise regime, his new diet, as well as the surgery itself had seemed to give him a renewed outlook on life.

As Brooke waved back at her grandmother, she lost track of who had the ball. Her attention on the game once again, she soon caught sight of Tessa running after Frisco. The dog seemed to know the three-year-old couldn't catch him unless he slowed. His trot changed to a walk and Tessa came up beside him, tagging him on the neck. Stopping immediately, he let the ball drop at her feet.

Tessa giggled, snatched up the ball and looked toward Brooke.

Brooke held out her hands. "Throw it, honey."

Tessa gave it an underhanded pitch that ended up to be a roll on the ground.

Scooping up the ball, still careful of her ankle, Brooke hurried away with it. Frisco and Tessa came after her and she managed to stay ahead of them. Suddenly a large hand capped her shoulder and she froze.

"Gotcha," Nate said in a puff of white vapor. His hand on her shoulder was electric and she knew he could feel the current, too. She was breathless from what she saw in his eyes. The cold was gone and replaced by desire that warmed every inch of her. They were both taking short, shallow breaths caused by whatever was zipping between them.

Taking the ball from Brooke's hand, Nate gave it a pitch toward Frisco.

The dog leaped up and caught it in midair.

When he brought it to Nate, Nate directed, "Play catch with Tessa for a bit," and he pointed to the little girl.

Obeying, Frisco trotted over to Tessa and dropped it at her feet.

Brooke encouraged her sister, "Throw it for him."

As Tessa took the ball and skittered it across the ground, Frisco chased it and Tessa was all smiles, clapping her hands and pointing to the ground at her feet. "Here. Here."

"I think Frisco could keep her occupied all day," Nate observed.

"She wanted to play ball with you, too, not just Frisco."

His attention turned to Brooke, and she felt every moment of his scrutiny. "What about you? You didn't seem happy to be at my door when you brought her over."

"It's just..." Brooke hesitated. "You hardly spoke to me yesterday at all. I wasn't sure you'd want anything to do with playing ball with us."

"You were busy yesterday." Somehow he managed to pull a curtain over the sparks of desire, and his response was curt, his jaw set.

"*Everyone* was busy yesterday," she returned. "And I think Mrs. Barlow really appreciated it. Dorothy Warner and one of the other women and I even managed to put together a couple of casseroles to freeze for her."

"She's lonely," Nate said.

"I know. I told her I'd bring Angel over to visit sometime soon."

Stuffing his hands in his jacket pockets, he mused, "I never thought of doing that with Frisco. Maybe we could organize a program—people with pets visiting elderly folk."

Tears almost welled in Brooke's eyes as she realized she and Nate were talking like they used to. They were talking as if they were friends again.

Nate must have realized it, too, and some of the guardedness came back into his expression. "You and Craig were pretty chummy while you were eating pizza last night. Are you going out sometime?" The question had no sooner hit the cold air than he held up his hand as if he'd remembered a previous comment she'd made. "Never mind. It isn't any of my business."

She couldn't let his conclusion go by without finding out how he was feeling about her. "Do you *want* it to be your business?"

"Whether I do or not really doesn't matter. You could take off again before the sun comes up."

As sadness filled her, she wished her life were different. "I wouldn't do that without a good reason."

"Maybe not. But I don't intend to spend time and effort on a relationship that won't go anywhere. I told you what I want, Brooke. I want exactly what I have here. Without any hubbub. Without anyone ever knowing who I was or who I am."

His voice was almost harsh, and she shouldn't have expected anything else from him. When she thought about her history with her father, with Tim... "And I don't fit into your picture."

"I wish you did." Now the harshness was gone and his voice was gravelly—as if the desire between them and everything they were losing troubled him deeply. "I wish you were just a normal veterinarian."

Although she might have had the same wish at times, right now anger unexpectedly bubbled to the surface...the anger that she'd known when Tim had rejected her. She lifted her chin, and her voice didn't expose the trembling she felt inside. "Well, I'm not normal, Nate. I'm not sure many people are. What I need in my life is a man who isn't afraid of what I have to offer, who can accept me exactly as I am, no matter what happens," she added. "But I guess I want the impossible. It seems that I always have."

Emotions tightened her throat, and she didn't want Nate to see how deeply she felt about him. "I think Tessa's been out here long enough. I'm going to take her inside."

When she turned and went to her sister, Nate didn't try to stop her. He simply whistled for Frisco while she corralled Tessa, then they all walked toward the house. Brooke was going to take her family out to dinner and then spend the rest of the evening alone…with Angel and a good book.

But that thought didn't satisfy her as it once might have.

It was cold and damp in Nate's garage on Monday evening. As he rubbed a chamois cloth over the red convertible he'd just waxed, he was unable to shake free of the heaviness that had dogged him ever since he'd put distance between himself and Brooke. He knew the distance was best, but telling himself that didn't seem to help the emptiness he was feeling.

If Brooke just wasn't so damn…damn…everything. She gave 100 percent of who she was to everything she did—to the animals she treated, to Tessa. That thought stopped him as he considered again the fact that he'd never even met, or wanted to meet, *his* half brother.

Cole Patterson, who was twenty-six now, symbolized the unhappiness Nate had known when his parents divorced. In Nate's estimation, Cole was the cause of his mother's and father's breakup and the secret they'd kept for so many years.

Before the scandal, Nate had always believed he and his father were best friends. He'd had the wind knocked out of him when the story had broken, and he hadn't gotten over the resentment of everything and everyone involved in it. He'd felt like a fool and an outsider...and still did.

The side door to the garage opened and Brooke stepped inside. When she saw Nate, she said, "Sorry. I didn't know you were here."

Tired of walking on eggshells with her, he growled, "There's nothing to be sorry about. Obviously, you needed something or you wouldn't have come in."

Her gaze went to the red sports car. "I wondered what was under that tarp."

Allowing his defensiveness to ease, he shrugged. "A remnant from my old life."

"You couldn't bear to part with it?" she asked with a smile.

"I suppose you could say that. I left everything behind *but* this. Maybe more than anything, I kept it as a reminder."

Brooke was wearing her wool jacket and corduroys. With her hair loose around her face, she looked prettier than she ever had. Her gaze ran over his navy sweatshirt and his black jeans. She looked at him the same way he looked at her, and he got hot just thinking about everything they could be together...do together.

As the silence stretched longer between them, she dropped her gaze from his and then motioned to the back of the garage. "I just came in to get something from my chest."

She had never explained what that chest was, and he was curious now. "Did you say it's your grandmother's?"

"It was. She gave it to me a few years ago. She intended it to be my hope chest."

So much about Brooke was unexpectedly traditional. "That's an old-fashioned concept."

"In a way, Granna's old-fashioned." Then, as if Brooke realized she was taking up his time, she moved toward the chest. "I won't bother you. I'll just get the scarves she embroidered and leave."

"She embroidered them?" Nate asked with surprise.

"She loves to do handwork in the evenings." Brooke went over to the chest, took a tiny key from her pocket and slipped it into the small lock. There was a soft click. She pocketed the key and then lifted the lid. The smell of cedar and linens wafted out, and it was a pleasant, homey odor in the cold garage.

Kneeling beside the chest, Brooke took out the top item.

When she saw Nate watching her, she said with a grin, "It's an apron. Granna said she knows women don't wear them anymore, but I should wear it when I make meals for special occasions."

"I guess that special occasion hasn't come up yet. It looks brand-new."

After she shifted the apron to the side of the chest, she riffled through other linens. "No, it hasn't come up yet." Delving deeper, she found the set of scarves, embroidered with pink and aqua flowers. A lace edge trimmed all of them.

Brooke lifted out two. "One for the nightstand and one for the coffee table. What do you think?"

As she unfolded the fabric, Nate could see all of the work, all of the hours of creativity that had gone into those scarves. "You only give scarves like that to someone you love very much," he said gruffly.

"I know. I might have always doubted if my dad loved me, but I never doubted if Granna did."

"Your dad looked good on Sunday."

"Yes, he did."

Nate caught the troubled look that passed over Brooke. "What's the matter?"

She hesitated, and he knew he hadn't given her reason to confide in him. "Is his condition still tenuous?"

"No. It's not that. The doctor told him if he keeps up with his diet and exercise routine and takes his medication, he'll be healthier than he has been in years. It's just— After his surgery, he asked me if I can forgive him—for leaving me...for all the years he wasn't there."

"What did you tell him?"

"I didn't give him an answer exactly. I don't want to tell him I can, if I don't *know* I can. I just said it might take some time."

"I know they say time heals all wounds." Nate shook his head. "Still, sometimes resentment festers instead of fading away."

After a few silent moments she asked, "Is that what happened with you?"

His gaze settled on the car, a symbol of what his life had been. "I don't know. I watch you with Tessa, and you don't seem to resent her at all."

"I don't. It's amazing, really. After Dad asked me to take care of her and I brought her back here with me, any jealousy I felt just vanished. Maybe because I'd always longed for a sister. Maybe because I'd always longed for someone to look at me the way she looks at me—as if I can keep her safe...as if she accepts me no matter what I do or what I say. Love is so unconditional coming from children."

"Until they're faced with reality," he argued. Once he knew about Cole, he didn't feel anything but anger at his father.

"Have you spent any time with your half brother?" Brooke asked, apparently knowing he was thinking about what had happened with his parents.

"I've never even met him." He expected her to say that was a shame. Or to criticize him for not making an effort. But she didn't.

As he gazed into her dark-brown eyes, he realized their conversation had become much too serious...and much too personal. Catching the sight of tulle sticking up from under what looked like another set of scarves, he asked, "What's that?"

Brooke shifted the linens and lifted a lace and tulle concoction. "It was my grandmother's wedding veil. It's beautiful, isn't it? The workmanship is so fine. It was handmade. Even if I never wear it, I'll always cherish it."

Unbidden, a picture flashed before Nate's eyes of Brooke wearing that veil...wearing a lace gown...walking down the aisle of a church with a bouquet of flowers in her hands. The idea startled him and he took a step back from the hope chest. "Why didn't you just leave the chest at your grandmother's, instead of lugging it around wherever you go?"

Carefully Brooke folded the veil again and settled it in the chest once more. "My grandmother gave it to me, and everything in that hope chest reminds me of her. It also reminds me of the reason why she gave it to me—that there's hope I'll settle down someday."

Despite the life Brooke had led, he could tell that her father might love to wander, but she would rather not. Still, she'd been dealt a hand that dictated the direction of her life, and there wasn't a lot she could do about it.

Brooke had repacked everything but the scarves when Nate was suddenly filled with the urge to give them both relief from what they were dealing with. He knew exactly how to accomplish that. "How would you like to take a ride with me?"

She rose to her feet and glanced at the sports car. "In that?"

"Yes, in that. I promise if I find a straight stretch of road I won't go over a hundred."

She looked taken aback for a moment, but then she saw his wide grin. "Make it eighty, and I'll buckle up beside you."

"You've got a deal."

Lifting the lid of the chest, she laid the scarves on the top. "I'll leave these here for safekeeping until we get back."

When she straightened again, Nate was close enough to her to see the golden flecks in her brown eyes...to inhale her lovely scent...to read the longing on her face that he felt, too. This woman was too special, and he couldn't pretend they were strangers when they weren't. Yet he knew friendship with her could dangerously lead him into much more.

"If we do this with the top down, your hair's going to blow," he warned her, unable to keep his hand at his side. He brushed his fingers lightly along her face and felt her tremble.

After a prolonged moment filled with everything neither could put into words, she said defiantly, "I don't care."

Pulling himself back from the brink of desire and a kiss that shouldn't happen, he caught her hand, grinned and tugged her toward the car. "We're going to have the ride of our lives."

On Tuesday evening, Nate was on his way out of his office to feed the animals in the kennel their supper when the phone on his desk buzzed. Returning to his desk to answer it, he sat on the corner.

Frisco settled on his haunches, looking up at his master expectantly.

"I promise this won't take long," he told the dog. "We'll feed our boarders, then go out for a good run."

Frisco cocked his head, listening to every word, and then stretched out on the floor to wait patiently.

"Who is it, Ellie?" he asked, as he picked up the receiver.

"It's your mother."

A pang of guilt stabbed Nate because he hadn't spoken to his mom in over a month. He knew she missed him. Muriel Stanton wished he had never left L.A. Every time he visited or phoned, she made that perfectly clear. He did wonder why she was calling him at the clinic, though.

Nate pushed line two, which was lit up. "Hi, Mom. How are you?"

"Better since I'm talking to you. I hope I'm not keeping you from anything important."

He glanced at Frisco. "Nothing that can't wait. Is something wrong?"

"No. Why?"

"Because you don't usually call at the clinic."

"I didn't want to leave a message on your machine and then have you ignore it. You're never home."

"That's not true, and you know it. I've been busy getting the house in order and settling in a new associate. I always return your calls."

"Sometimes it's a day or two," she protested.

Nate sighed. "If you tell me it's an emergency, I promise to call you back right away."

There was a long pause. "I miss the sound of your

voice, Nate. Talking over the telephone isn't the same thing as seeing you in person.''

"I saw you at Christmas.''

"That's not the same as knowing you're in the vicinity. And now that you've built that house…"

"I'll still come back to visit.''

"That's why I'm calling.''

Uh-oh. He hadn't seen that one coming.

"Your father said he'd phoned you about coming out for the telethon this weekend. And you said you were too busy. Are you really?''

That note in his mother's voice always got to him…the note that said a mother's love was unconditional and forever, no matter what kind of rocky road they'd traveled. "I did tell him I was too busy for the same reasons I just mentioned to you.''

"He thinks you're making excuses, that you don't want to see us.''

His relationship with his parents was so complicated now because he still felt betrayed by their years of secrecy. "I'm not making excuses. I do have a lot going on.''

"Are you sure you can't come just for a few days? Just the weekend, maybe? I have something to tell you, and I'd like to do it in person. Besides that… I just want you to come. We need to sit down together, talk as we haven't since…since you left. Maybe we can lay it all to rest.''

Could they? Could he shed his resentment and not dread going back to L.A.? "Let me think about it. I promise I'll call you tomorrow evening.''

Satisfied with that for the moment, his mother told him to take care of himself and then insisted she wouldn't take up any more of his time, making him feel guilty as hell.

He was just hanging up the phone when Brooke peeked into his office. "Do you want me to feed our boarders?"

Last night when he'd taken Brooke for a ride in his convertible, he'd had such a good time. The stars, the wind, the speed, Brooke beside him, had given him a sense of well-being he hadn't experienced in a long time. When they'd returned to the garage, it had taken every ounce of his self-control not to kiss her. But he'd managed it. She'd gone to her apartment and he'd gone back to his house. Once there, though, even with Frisco at his feet, he'd felt alone.

Now he raised his gaze to Brooke's, bracing himself for the impact of her soul-deep beauty...her presence. "I almost forgot about the boarders. That phone call—"

"Is something wrong?" She came deeper into the office.

"No. It was my mother this time, asking me to come out for the telethon this weekend. I think she wants all of us to make peace."

"Is that what you want?"

"I want back what we used to have. But I don't see how that's possible. And when I think of the cocktail party before the telethon, the telethon, dinner afterward—" Suddenly he stopped. "How would you like to go with me?"

"You're kidding!"

The idea took form, and he grabbed on to it. He wanted to make the effort to reconcile everything that had happened, but he suddenly knew having Brooke with him would make the trip much easier. "No, I'm not. We could leave Friday morning, come back late Saturday night. The Flagstaff Clinic will cover for me. I've covered enough for them."

"What about Angel and Frisco?"

"When I went to L.A. over Christmas, Ellie took care of Frisco for me. She probably wouldn't mind spoiling Angel, too. Why don't you ask her? I'm sure she'll be honest about it. I'll cover your fare if you're concerned about that."

"I don't know, Nate. What will your parents think?"

"They'll think I'm bringing a friend. We *are* friends, aren't we, Brooke?"

Her eyes took on a luminous quality that told him about something deeper than friendship. The same desire he felt? The wish that everything between them could be simpler?

"Yes, we're friends. If you really want me to go—"

"I really want you to go. Have you ever been to L.A.?"

"No. I always thought that someday...someday I'd see the Pacific Ocean."

"We can make it happen. We can drive to the beach Saturday morning before the telethon. That'll give me the bolstering I'll need to get through the day."

"Did you ever think you might enjoy your visit?" she teased with a grin.

"I can only hope. I'll call and make reservations. But first I'm going to feed our boarders, and then I'm going to take Frisco for a run. Are you finished for the day?"

"Before she left, Ellie told me some test results are in. I'm going to go over those first," Brooke explained.

As they walked into the hall together, Frisco trailing behind them, Nate caught Brooke's elbow. When she looked up at him, he was filled with the urge to keep her close to him...always. Bending, he kissed her forehead. "Thanks for agreeing to go with me. It means a lot."

Her eyes shimmered, and her smile was radiant as she admitted, "It means a lot to me, too. I just wish..." She dropped her gaze and shook her head. "Never mind. Go feed our furry friends before they riot."

Pulling away from him, she headed to the counter in the reception area.

He knew what she wished. She wished she was normal. She wished she could stay. She wished all the same things he did.

Excitement filled Brooke as she went behind the desk and found the folder Ellie had left for her.

California with Nate. Almost two whole days with him—really being with him. She couldn't get too excited. She had to be practical....

Focusing her attention on the matters at hand, she opened the folder and read the lab results on Cinders, Mr. McNeill's schnauzer.

When the clinic door opened, she stopped her analysis and looked up. There was a gentleman standing there, who looked to be in his early thirties. He was good-looking, in a casual sort of way with his black wire-rimmed glasses, a heavy denim jacket and khakis. She'd never seen him before. "May I help you?"

"I'm looking for Dr. Pennington."

Something in the way he said it made her heart beat faster with concern. "I'm Brooke Pennington."

He extended a hand to her and she shook it.

"It's good to meet you. I'm Jack Warner, Jenny's father."

Relief swept over Brooke, and she smiled. "Jenny's a wonderful little girl."

His smile was wide, too. "She sure is." He seemed to pause for effect, then went on. "She told me something interesting."

"What was that?" Brooke expected a story about Angel or—

"She insists that Biscuit's leg was broken and that you healed it. Not in the usual way a vet heals, but in some *unusual* way."

Brooke kept silent.

When she didn't fill the void, he did. "I'm not just Jenny's father, Dr. Pennington. I'm a reporter with the *Whisper Rock Chronicle*. This would make a wonderful human interest story."

Brooke's whole life shook and her heart shouted, *No. Not now. Not again.* If this reporter found out the truth, she'd have to leave Whisper Rock. Calming herself, she said softly, "Mr. Warner, little girls have very big imaginations. I simply calmed Biscuit so I could examine her, and I discovered that her injury wasn't that serious."

Warner's brows arched and his mouth twisted wryly. "That's the story my wife told me—something about a kink and a chiropractor. But Jenny's pretty savvy, even though she's only ten. She often sees things my wife misses."

"Your wife didn't miss anything. She was in the same room with me."

"Yes. But Jenny said you had the dog on the counter, not on the table, and your back was turned to them."

Afraid because of the details he knew, frustrated because he wouldn't accept her explanation, she relied on her professional demeanor to hold steady. "Look, Mr. Warner. I don't want to be rude, but I have to go over these lab reports. Biscuit wasn't seriously injured. That's all there was to it."

He eyed her for a long time. "That's what I thought you'd say. Of course, I can't prove otherwise. But I'll be keeping my ears open for other stories like this one. If I hear of another one, I'll be back.''

After the clinic door closed once again, Brooke sagged against the counter. Tears filled her eyes as she thought about how much she'd been looking forward to going to L.A. with Nate, her hope that he could look past everything but their feelings for each other.

Now this.

She'd have to watch her step. She'd have to be extra careful. Most of all, she'd have to enjoy every minute she had with Nate as if it were her last.

Chapter Nine

Brooke's trip to L.A. swept her into a life that was a world away from Whisper Rock, the veterinary clinic and the reporter who could write an article that might again change the course of her life. To her surprise, Perry Stanton sent a chauffeured limousine to the airport. It was a delight for her to ride in the sumptuous vehicle, but Nate became more somber as the chauffeur sped by walled and gated estates in Bel Air, finally turning into a property surrounded by ornate wrought iron. The chauffeur stopped, exited the limousine and pressed a button on the intercom at the entrance. In a few moments the tall gates swung open, and the limousine headed toward Nate's former home.

The concrete drive led up to a house that didn't shout with fantastic opulence, but rather spoke of understated wealth. Mediterranean style, it was fashioned of cream stucco with a red barrel-tiled roof and wrought-iron balconies. Granite steps with ornate planters on either side led to the massive arched mahogany door.

"This is beautiful, Nate," Brooke murmured as the chauffeur fetched their suitcases from the limo.

As if he were trying to see it through her eyes, Nate gazed at the house for a moment and then said, "I suppose it is. My dad talked about moving to a smaller place after he and my mother divorced, but he never did. I thought it was because there were too many memories here that he didn't want to forget. But after the tabloid story broke..." Nate shrugged. "I figured he stayed here because it was a symbol of who he was, and his status in the industry. My mother and I lived in a two-bedroom cottage in Malibu after the divorce. She's always loved the ocean. It was my dad's getaway when they were married."

The massive, front door swung open and Perry Stanton himself stood there looking down at them. "It's good to see you, son," he said immediately. Then he addressed Brooke. "And it's good to meet you, Dr. Pennington. Nate has spoken highly of you."

Perry Stanton was as old-world charming in person as he was on screen. There was a courtly quality about him that would make any woman stand up and take notice. Brooke had thought she'd be in awe of the man but now realized she just wanted to get to know him to learn more about Nate. "It's good to be here, sir."

He made a face and dismissed the title immediately. "It's Perry, Dr. Pennington. May I call you Brooke?"

"Of course you can," she said with a smile, and she felt Nate stiffen beside her. When she glanced at him, his jaw was set and she could see the tension in his stance.

"You've had a long trip. Please come in and meet Nate's mother." Perry gestured inside to the foyer, expecting them to follow.

"I didn't think Mom would be here until the cocktail

party tonight,'' Nate said, as they climbed the steps and met his father in the Mexican-tiled foyer.

A beautiful woman in her midfifties rushed toward them. Her ash-blond hair was secured in a twist at the back of her head and her emerald-green pantsuit showed off her still-svelte figure. She hugged Nate immediately. ''It's so good to see you.'' After she held on for a few moments, she released her son and turned to Brooke. ''You must be Brooke. I'm so glad you've joined Nate's practice. He was working much too hard.''

''It's good to meet you, Mrs. Stanton.'' Brooke could see the obvious affection emanating from her for her son.

''Please call me Muriel. I'd like to chat with you a bit, but why don't I show you to your rooms first. We can sit by the pool afterward and get to know each other better before the guests start arriving.''

''If you'll excuse me, I have a few calls to make,'' Perry said. ''I'll meet you by the pool.''

Nate was silent as they climbed the wide, marble stairway. Brooke noticed the valuable artwork on the walls. Everything was so tastefully arranged, not in the least bit overdone. As Muriel explained who the guests would be at the cocktail party that evening, she also described the advantages of the new cancer wing she and other benefactors wanted to build for children.

She was passionate about it, and as she motioned Brooke to a pretty room decorated in pale blue and yellow, she blushed. ''It's a cause I hold dear,'' she explained. ''My sister died of cancer when she was only five. The advances made since then are wonderful.'' She glanced at her son. ''Nate's heard me go on about this before, so I'm sure I'm boring him.''

''You never bore me, Mom,'' he said with a quick

smile for her. Then he turned serious again. "Are you going to be Dad's hostess tonight?"

Her cheeks became rosier. "Yes, I am. He asked for my help organizing the party, and you know how I love to do this kind of thing." Changing the subject, she gestured to the room across the hall. "You'll be in that room, Nate. I thought you might want to be close to Brooke."

As her gaze passed from one to the other, neither of them spoke. She continued on as if the silence meant nothing at all. "Just make yourselves at home. I'll see you both downstairs after you've changed." His mother left then, a trace of her expensive perfume floating behind her.

After the chauffeur brought up their suitcases and left them in their rooms, he tipped his hat to them and disappeared down the staircase.

"Your parents are very nice," Brooke offered, hoping the sky-blue sheath she'd brought would be appropriate for the cocktail party. "I was worried that they would think I was—"

"What?"

"I don't know. Out of my depth here?"

Nate examined her closely. "It doesn't matter what they think of you, Brooke. Unless you're trying to impress my father."

"Why would I want to do that?"

"Any woman who's around Perry Stanton usually tries to impress him."

She remembered then what Nate had said about women dating him to get to know his father. "You know me better than that, don't you?"

All of the tension of the past two weeks hummed between them. Then he let out a breath and seemed to relax a bit. "Yes, I guess I do. Coming back here is always a culture shock. I've gotten used to my life in Whisper Rock.''

"This weekend *could* be fun," she said lightly.

"I guess it could be. But I'm getting the feeling that something else is going on that I don't know about.''

She was hesitant to approach the subject on her mind, but she did, anyway. ''What did you tell your parents about us?''

"I didn't tell them anything. My mother just assumed since I brought you along that we were sleeping together. She put us in separate rooms for appearances' sake. Appearances are all-important to her. They always have been. But I'll set her straight if you want me to.''

"No. I…''

The space between them diminished as Nate stepped closer. Sliding his fingers under her hair, he tilted her chin up. "It about drives me nuts to be close to you and not want more than—'' He broke off and swore, then asked, "Do you know how hard it will be for me tonight not to come across that hall?''

"Nate,'' she murmured in a voice filled with as much desire and longing as she saw in his eyes.

When he bent his head, he didn't just take a kiss. He seduced her lips with his tongue until she opened them. Then he thrust inside as if he belonged. He did belong, and she wanted to belong to him.

As the kiss went deeper, he explored more thoroughly. His hand found her breast, and she didn't move away. This is what she wanted with Nate. She wanted him touching her and kissing her. She wanted him in her life twenty-four hours a day, seven days a week. She wanted so many things she couldn't even name—things that began with everlasting and ended with forever. In her dreams she saw herself in her grandmother's wedding veil and Nate in a tuxedo. Yet when she awakened, she knew the images belonged in a fantasy.

With a rough oath he pulled away from her. "That's what happens when I get too close to you. Tonight you'd better lock your bedroom door."

Boldness she didn't know she possessed led her to shake her head. "I'm not going to lock the door, Nate."

The muscle in his jaw worked. "Because you trust me? Or because you want an affair that can't go anywhere?"

Because she loved him. But she couldn't tell him that. She was afraid he'd back away from her for good. Why was she courting heartache? Hadn't she been abandoned often enough? Nate, with his abhorrence of rumors, gossip and the limelight could never seriously accept her in his life.

When she didn't answer, he pulled her to him and kissed her hard again. Then he set her away.

When he went into his room and closed the door, they both knew why. She wasn't "normal." Not only would she bring too many complications into his life, but she couldn't promise him she'd stay.

A half hour later Nate kept glancing at Brooke as they sat with his parents around a black wrought-iron table under a yellow-and-white-striped umbrella. If he'd had trouble keeping his hands off Brooke before, it was almost impossible now. She was wearing a blue sheath with tiny straps. Her arms were bare. Her legs were beautifully curved, and in high heels she was a knockout. He couldn't keep his eyes off her. It seemed she couldn't keep hers off him, either. He was wearing a charcoal suit that had been custom-made. He wasn't sure if bringing Brooke along had been the smartest thing he'd ever done or the most foolish. Although she was a great buffer with his parents, keeping the conversation rolling without him having to say much, she was an irresistible temptation he couldn't indulge in.

"It's a shame the two of you can't stay longer than tomorrow night," Muriel Stanton said after a momentary lull in the conversation. Her black dress and pearls were her standard cocktail party dress.

"Getting away from the clinic for more than a day or two is difficult, Mom. You know that."

"Yes, I suppose it is. I just wish..." She looked at Nate's father, and the two of them exchanged a glance that told Nate in no uncertain terms that the two of them were planning something.

Perry hadn't changed into his tux yet but was still dressed in a polo shirt and casual slacks. Now he patted his ex-wife's hand. "Go ahead and tell him. You know you can't wait."

"Tell me what?" Nate asked.

As Muriel leaned closer to Nate's father, he gently squeezed her fingers. "We didn't want to tell you over the phone. Your father and I...we've decided to remarry. We're planning the ceremony for the week after Easter, and we're hoping you can return then. Will you?"

Shocked, Nate tried to absorb what his mother had said. Since the divorce, there had been tension between his mother and father, although they'd always been civil for his sake, he'd supposed. Now, however, there wasn't any tension. What had happened? How could his mother forget about the hurt his father had caused her? How could she forget about the other woman and the other child?

"Aren't you going to congratulate us?" Perry pressed. "We're going to announce our plans on the telethon tomorrow."

That did it. Anger roiled inside of Nate and he stood. "Mom, can I talk to you in private for a few minutes?"

Perry frowned. "Anything you have to say—"

Muriel clasped her ex-husband's shoulder. "It's all right. Why don't you and Brooke get another drink? Nate and I will talk in the rose garden."

A few minutes later, Nate ignored the ornate bench by the billowing fountain, too agitated to sit. "Do you know what you're doing, Mom?"

She didn't hesitate for a moment. "I love your father. I always have."

"But he cheated on you! He had a child with another woman. How can you just forget all of that?"

"Oh, Nate." His mother shook her head. "I'll *never* forget any of it. But your dad and I have decided we need each other. We still have feelings after all these years. We've both dated plenty of other people, but no other man can fill your father's shoes for me."

All too well Nate had seen how the divorce had torn his mother apart. He'd heard her crying in the middle of the night and had seen the evidence of her tears and her ravished emotions in the morning. He hadn't known what it was all about, because they hadn't told him. They'd simply said they'd grown apart...that his dad's career with his long absences made marriage impossible. As a child, Nate had accepted that explanation.

Then three years ago he'd found out the truth, and his opinion of his father had changed. "What makes you think dad won't do it again?" he asked harshly, wondering if his mother was facing reality.

"If you think I haven't looked at this from all angles, you're wrong. I know who your father is. I know millions of women idolize him. But as he's aged, he's matured. He tells me there will never be anyone else."

"Why do you think you can believe him?"

"You and your father were best friends for years, Nate. After the scandal broke you hardly spoke to him. He's the same man he was *before* you learned about his affair. Yes, he has flaws. But we all have flaws. I've forgiven him for what happened. If you don't do the same, the two of you will never have the relationship you once had."

Still feeling betrayed, as if he didn't know his father at all, he decided, "That relationship is gone forever."

His mother clasped his arm. "Nate, we're sorry your engagement broke up because of the scandal. But that was the reporters' fault, not ours. You're blaming us for it."

Was he? Was he using his parents as scapegoats? He didn't think so. "No, I'm not blaming you for what happened with Linda. But I *am* blaming you for keeping a secret all those years that affected me, too. I'm happy for you, Mom, if this is what you want. But—"

When Nate felt a hand on his shoulder, he turned around and faced his father. Brooke was standing a few feet behind, and he suspected she thought he might need reinforcements.

"It's what we both want, son. And we want you to be a part of our lives again. We want to be a family again."

"Do you want Cole to be a part of this family, too?" Nate asked bluntly.

His parents exchanged a look.

With shoulders straight, her head high, his mother admitted, "I've accepted Cole. He's your father's son. He's your brother. You should accept him, too."

As Nate looked at his mom and his dad, he knew that he loved them. But he was still disappointed with his father and felt betrayed by both of them. For the past three years they hadn't even hinted that they were going to reconcile. Fortunately, this time they'd told him themselves instead of letting him read it in a tabloid. "You've thrown a lot at me. I need time to absorb it."

"Maybe you and I can have a drink alone before everyone arrives tonight," Perry suggested.

He didn't want to remain angry with his father, but he didn't think the resentment would fade by willing it away. Still, he had to try.

"All right, Dad. But for now..." He caught Brooke's gaze. "Would you like to take a walk around the property?"

She nodded.

When Nate took Brooke's hand, he felt as if it belonged in his, he felt as if she grounded him. She not only excited him, she brought him calm and peace. He needed that right now.

As they strolled away from his parents, he didn't talk, and neither did she. He realized she understood silence, too. She seemed to understand everything.

What happens when she leaves? an inner voice asked him.

He'd deal with that when the time came. For now he just wanted to be with her. For now he wouldn't think about tomorrow.

Nate took Brooke to the beach to see the Pacific Ocean on Saturday morning. Walking on the sand with him, seeing the Pacific for the first time, had been an experience she would never forget. Although Nate hadn't kissed her, she'd felt closer to him than she ever had. But neither of them spoke of the emotions and desire so near the surface.

After they drove into the city, they experienced most of the telethon from the audience seats in the TV studio. Brooke watched Perry Stanton, as emcee, work his magic as he spoke with children who had cancer, drawing out their stories. He pleaded persuasively for money. The cameras often panned the star-studded gallery, who were answering phones. For a few hours that afternoon, she and Nate manned phones in the back—off-camera. Although Nate offered to take her sight-seeing instead of staying in the studio, she'd replied she didn't think she could find any sights more interesting than where they were.

It was almost five and nearing the end of the telethon when Nate leaned close and murmured in her ear, "I told Dad we'd meet him in the back."

Nate's breath was warm on her cheek. All day she'd been so aware of him, as she suspected he was of her. At the beach, she'd wanted him to take her into his arms and make love to her with the ocean roaring in the background. But that was just another fantasy because Nate was mightily fighting the desire sparking between them. Now as they stood and his hand rested possessively at her waist to guide her through the maze of cameras, cables and people, she wished she had the freedom to take his hand...to lean close to him and kiss him...to feel as if she really belonged with him.

They'd reached the area where the off-camera phone staff was still taking calls, when Nate stopped suddenly to stare up at the video monitor. He could hear his father's voice through the speakers as Perry Stanton invited his ex-wife on stage with him. Then he made the announcement of their plans to remarry.

"I wonder if he thinks that'll pull in more donations," Nate muttered.

"Maybe he simply wanted to make the announcement before gossip columnists and tabloids could get hold of the news."

Her soft words brought Nate's gaze to her. "I suppose

that's true. But it won't stop the reporters from wanting more. You can never give them enough.''

A tall, good-looking, dark-haired man who appeared to be in his twenties came into the area then and seemed to be looking for someone. Brooke wondered if he was one of those reporters.

A few moments later Perry and Muriel Stanton walked through the doorway from the stage, their faces beaming. When they caught sight of Brooke and Nate they came toward them. At the same time Perry waved the gentleman Brooke had been watching over to their circle.

He capped the young man on the shoulder. ''Nate, this is someone I want you to meet. Cole Patterson, Nate, my other son. Nate, this is your half brother. Your mother and I invited him to come to dinner with us. We thought you two should finally get to know each other.''

Brooke saw the set of Nate's shoulders square; his spine become rigidly straight. There was a tension in him that had been there all weekend but was now magnified tenfold.

However, he seemed to recover from the shock of being confronted with the situation in public, and he extended his hand. ''Hello, Cole.''

There was no warmth in his voice, just a politeness that he might use greeting any stranger. Brooke realized that was what Cole was—a stranger, a stranger who had taken Nate's dad away from him. At least, that's the way he might see it, Brooke supposed, remembering everything she'd thought and felt when Granna had told her that Tessa had been born.

Immediately Cole returned the handshake with an easy smile. ''It's good to finally meet you. Dad told me you're a veterinarian somewhere in Arizona.''

Nate's mouth tightened with Cole's use of the term

Dad. "Yes, I am," he said evenly. Then he motioned to Brooke. "This is Brooke Pennington, an associate of mine."

After Brooke and Cole murmured hellos, Nate turned to his father. "We'd better get going to dinner, since Brooke and I are catching a late flight tonight."

Muriel's gaze passed over her son with concern. "I thought maybe once we introduced Cole to you... Are you sure you and Brooke can't at least stay until tomorrow?" she asked again.

"Mom, I told you. We have to get back to the clinic."

Perry Stanton looked disappointed, but he accepted Nate's decision. "I have reservations at a new place in the hills. I'm sure you'll like it. We can get going as soon as I—"

Suddenly there was a shout from the far end of the studio. Seconds later two men with cameras rushed over. Cole didn't seem perturbed, and neither did Perry Stanton as one of the men, obviously a reporter, demanded, "Just one picture, Perry, of your whole family. We've never gotten one of those." The words were hardly out of his mouth when a flash went off from the other photographer's camera.

Grabbing Brooke's hand, Nate muttered a raging curse. To his mother he yelled, "Use my cell phone number." Then he yanked Brooke along with him, slipping behind a partition. Soon he led her through a door and down a hallway.

"Won't they follow?" she asked breathlessly as she rushed beside him.

"No. I know my way out of here. It's like a maze. Besides, they'll stay with Dad and get the sure thing, rather than chasing after me. I'm old news. His remarriage to Mom and the story about Cole being his son are more recent. I just can't believe Dad didn't tell me Cole was going to dinner with us.''

''Maybe he was afraid you wouldn't go, too.''

Nate stopped and faced her. ''I hate secrets, Brooke. Dad's done nothing but keep them for years. All of them have ended up disrupting my life.''

As they wended their way down another hall and through another door, Brooke thought about the secret she was keeping from him. Should she tell him about Jenny's father coming to the office?

What good would it do?

She'd just have to be careful. For the first time in her life, she was actually thinking of denying her gift, turning her back on any healing energy that came her way. Would that prove her love to Nate? Would he be able to let his feelings for her grow if she told him she would deny her gift?

Nate's cell phone rang, and he plucked it off his belt with a scowl.

Brooke could tell it was Nate's dad.

''All right. We'll meet you at the west entrance. Dad, I don't appreciate the way you handled this.''

A few moments went by as Nate listened.

''I don't care if Cole *did* want the picture. He's an entertainment lawyer. Why wouldn't he? But it's not for me anymore. You know that. No one in Whisper Rock knows who I am, and I want to keep it that way. Are you sure the reporters took off?''

There was another pause.

''We'll exit from the side door and watch for your car. But if anybody follows us to the restaurant, Brooke and I are leaving.''

Attaching the phone once more to his belt, Nate plowed

his hand through his hair. "Five minutes. We're meeting them outside."

"The reporters got pictures?"

"Of my mother and dad and Cole. Not quite a family portrait," Nate said bitterly. "But it will have to do. Come on. Let's get this over with so I can get back to my life in Whisper Rock."

Night hadn't faded into light yet as Nate carried Brooke's suitcase up the stairs to her apartment early Sunday morning. She followed him, wishing she could ease his turmoil. He'd been reluctant to talk during their return trip, and she hadn't pushed him. Dinner with his parents and Cole had been tense. If Nate was going to get to know his brother, he had to spend time with him alone, not under the scrutiny of Perry and Muriel Stanton. She never could have let her own feelings for Tessa blossom as they had if Granna and her dad had been watching.

She realized now after seeing Nate with his family, that she *had* to forgive her dad. It wasn't only the *right* thing to do, it was the *best* thing to do. Cal Pennington had done the best he could, just as Perry and Muriel Stanton had. Just like everyone else, her father was human and made mistakes. She could keep blaming him for those mistakes, or she could forgive him and maybe they could really begin being father and daughter.

Nate used his key to open the apartment door. As he let Brooke precede him inside, she realized how much she liked coming back here. "It seems odd not having Angel running to say hello."

"Same here. When I go back to the house, it'll seem empty without Frisco. After we both catch a few hours' sleep we'll round them up. They probably had a blast with Ellie."

After Nate deposited Brooke's suitcase on her bed, he faced her. "Thanks for going with me this weekend. I know it wasn't a picnic for you, but I appreciated you being there."

Unbuttoning her coat, she slid it off and draped it on a kitchen chair. "Your family isn't so different from any other."

"Oh, no?" he drawled with disbelief.

"No. Are you going to fly out for your mom and dad's wedding? Maybe you and Cole could really get a chance to talk."

"Maybe I don't want a chance to talk. Maybe I just want to leave the whole mess in L.A. and live my life here."

"That doesn't sound like you."

He approached her slowly. "Maybe you don't know me."

"I *do* know you, Nate. You're big-hearted and considerate, and you don't like to leave anything unfinished."

His gaze searched her face, and then he clasped her shoulders. "I think I want to forget all of it for now."

A light was in his eyes that warmed her to her core, that drew her toward him, that sparked hunger as she'd never known. Still, she tried to think straight. "It will just be there later. It will just—"

"Keep quiet, Brooke," he ordered. Then he made sure she did.

His lips pressed to hers in a demand that couldn't be denied. His tongue swept her mouth until she couldn't think *or* breathe. A few moments later he was lifting her and carrying her to the bed. Shrugging out of his jacket, he came down beside her and began unbuttoning her blouse. His gaze sought hers, and she didn't protest or even think about pushing him away.

Obviously reading the hunger and need in her eyes, too, his voice was a husky murmur as he said, "I want you, Brooke." He kissed her brow, her nose, her cheek and the pulse point on her neck. His lips kept traveling downward until they met her bra. "I want to undress you," he rasped.

"I want to undress *you*," she replied, giving him permission, needing him, wanting him now, if she couldn't have him tomorrow.

Once he'd ridded her of her blouse and her bra, his lips scalded her skin, taunted her breasts, created a yearning so deep she didn't think it could ever be fulfilled. Yet she knew it could—by Nate.

As much as she wanted him to touch her, she wanted to touch him. His skin was so taut, his muscles so defined, the heat of his body so fascinating. After he'd tossed his shirt aside, she ran her fingers through his chest hair. He groaned and sucked in a breath. "Brooke," he growled, catching her hands. "It seems as if I've wanted you for so long. Too long. I don't know if I can hold on."

"I want you now, Nate."

The aching feeling in her voice and on her face must have convinced him. He reached for the button on her slacks and was unfastening them when she remembered how much he didn't like secrets. She had to tell him…

"Nate, I'm a virgin," she whispered.

His hands stilled at once.

She went on, "I just thought you should know. It doesn't matter. I want you." *I love you,* she thought, unable to say the words aloud.

With a muttered epithet, he rolled away from her and pushed himself to the side of the bed. "It *does* matter, Brooke. It matters a hell of a lot."

"Why?" she managed.

"Because I won't be your first if I can't be your last. I don't know what I thought I was doing here. Maybe using you as a release from all the pent-up frustration of the trip. I won't do that to either of us."

Tears came to Brooke's eyes as she realized Nate wasn't only a considerate man, he was a noble one.

Pulling his shirt on, he stood and let it hang out over his jeans.

She couldn't let him leave like this. It was an end, not a beginning, and she didn't want that. Scrambling into her blouse, letting her bra lie on the bed, she ran to him as he picked up his coat to go. "What if I said I'd stay? What if I told you I wouldn't use my gift? I'd just practice regular veterinary medicine?"

The world stopped as Nate stood frozen. Finally he said, "You can't just turn it on and off."

She let out the breath she'd been holding. "No, I can't. But I don't have to go with it. I can break the energy circuit. I don't have to accept it. I don't have to be an instrument. I can just be a regular vet."

He must have seen all the emotion swirling inside her because he murmured, "Oh, Brooke. That can't be my decision. It has to be yours. You can't give anyone else a responsibility like that."

She realized that was true. Still, she had to know... "But *would* it make a difference?"

The electricity that always hung between them seemed to crackle ferociously. It was as if hope was in the air, and they could both feel it and almost touch it. "Yes, it would make a difference. But I think you're too dedicated and gifted to be a regular vet, even if that's what you want."

"Nate…"

Holding up his hand, he stopped her. "We're both exhausted. We both want what we probably can't have."

He was right about the exhaustion. She needed a couple of hours' sleep before she could think clearly again.

"I told Ellie I'd pick up Angel and Frisco around four. Do you want to come along?"

"Why don't you pick them up and I'll make supper for us? Then maybe we can talk some more."

His mouth twisted in a wry smile. "I don't think either of us has talking on our mind, but that sounds like a good idea." He pushed her hair behind her ear, then gently brushed his fingers down the side of her face. "I'll be back after I pick up our pets."

Nate left her apartment, leaving her with hope about their future but with a heaviness in her heart that came from thinking about giving up her gift.

It was a decision she didn't want to have to make.

Chapter Ten

After Nate left, Brooke unpacked, drew the blinds, then undressed and slipped into bed. She could still feel his kisses...still feel the branding possessiveness of his touches. Although she was exhausted, she lay there for a long while thinking about the decision she had to make, thinking about what would happen tonight, what Nate might say and do. Finally she slipped into sleep, where she dreamed...of him.

When she awakened she felt disoriented and glanced at the bedside clock. It was 2:00 p.m. She should shower and get supper going so it would be ready when Nate arrived. Her decision was made. She loved Nate. She needed to belong to him. She could use everything she'd learned to practice veterinary medicine. Her heart skipped when she thought about not using extraordinary means and denying her gift. Closing her eyes, she could see herself practicing beside Nate...having a life with him.

As Brooke showered, dressed and began supper, she felt happy, almost light. She'd make vegetable soup, a tofu and couscous casserole and cornbread. Slowly she would introduce Nate to everything she liked best about vegetarian cooking.

She'd been working in the kitchen for about an hour when there was a knock on the apartment door. The sky was gray again, heavy with clouds that predicted more snow. She turned on the living room light on her way to answer the door. Maybe Nate had gone to Ellie's early. She couldn't wait to see Angel again, hold her, pet her—

When Brooke opened the door, her smile faded and fear gripped her heart.

Jack Warner was standing there, and he held a manila envelope in his hand. "May I come in?" he asked, his expression serious.

"I'd rather you didn't. I'm making supper and—"

"I know where you went this weekend. I know who Nate Stanton is. There are a few things we need to discuss."

Her insides trembled and her palms became damp as she stood aside to let him enter, then closed the door behind him. "What do you want?" she asked almost in a whisper.

"Look, Dr. Pennington. There's no reason to be frightened. You have nothing to fear from me if you tell me the truth."

He was right. She *was* frightened. Not of him, but of everything he could do to her dreams. He could destroy them. "And just what will you do with my truth, Mr. Warner?"

His serious expression gave way to a smile. "I'm going to make my career."

"At our expense. Nate and I have a right to have our own lives. Private lives."

"You know, I only wanted to know where *you* went

over the weekend because I was just planning the article about *you*. See, I found this other write-up." He took a newspaper clipping from the envelope.

Brooke knew exactly what it was. It was the article from the Chicago paper that had ended her relationship with Tim. Just to make sure he wasn't bluffing, she glanced at it. He had highlighted some sentences and underlined others.

Tapping on it with his forefinger, he said, "I know this story is big, bigger than the space this paper gave to it. So I followed you this weekend. My hunch was worth the price of a ticket. Where do you think it led me? Straight to the gates of Perry Stanton's mansion. Holy smokes! I hadn't just stumbled on one story, but one very great big story. Nate Stanton had a following of his own. Imagine the headline—Son of Movie Screen Idol Involved with Healer."

"You wouldn't do that." She was hoping beyond hope, hoping the sweetness she'd seen in Jenny somehow had been handed down from her father.

"Wouldn't do that?" he asked with a short laugh. "I've been writing articles for the *Whisper Rock Chronicle* for five years. We settled here because my wife's family is here. But do you think I want to *stay* here? This story could get me a real reporter's job. I'm just like every husband and father out there. I want financial security for my family. This could lead me straight to it."

She stepped away from the article as if it would bite her. "How could you live with yourself if your financial security destroys our lives?"

"You're exaggerating. Once this story hits about the two of you, Nate will have more business in his clinic than he can handle. He'll have to turn it away."

"You don't understand. Nate doesn't want that. That's why he moved here."

"To get away from the scandal? Yeah, I figured that out from the time line. Do you know why he chose Whisper Rock?"

Suddenly she realized she was doing exactly what the reporter wanted her to do—giving him information. That was a mistake. "I'm not going to tell you anything. You won't have anything to print." She was trying desperately to hold on to the dream she'd woven since last night—the dream of her and Nate having a life together.

"You're naive if you believe that. I've got enough just from my little trip to L.A. Everyone knew about Perry Stanton's telethon, and I figured that's why you two had gone out there. I was even in the audience at the studio watching the two of you. I saw that scene with the reporters, the way Nate didn't want anything to do with the family picture." He paused. "Or his half brother. You don't think I have enough?"

"He could sue you. *I* could sue you."

"You don't know how to threaten realistically, Dr. Pennington. If everything I print is the truth—what's already in print, what I heard and what I saw—there's nothing you can do about it."

She could see there was no talking to this man. There was no way she could convince him to leave her and Nate alone. He'd put the time and expense into finding out about them, and he wanted to cash in on it. A heavy weight settled over her as she realized she had to save Nate from this. She couldn't put him through another circus. She couldn't let the spotlight of unwanted, public attention cause upheaval to his life again. If she stayed in Whisper Rock, the story would become bigger than both of them. Nate would hate her for causing it, and she wouldn't be able to bear seeing the resentment in his eyes. On the other hand, if she left and no one could find her, the story might hit it big, but it would die down. A day, maybe two, and everyone would forget about it…and her. She hadn't been here that long. She hadn't attracted attention. All she had to do was hole up somewhere for a few weeks and then start her life over…again. Only, this time she knew she'd be lonelier than she'd ever been. This time she'd feel as if she were leaving her heart and soul behind.

Crossing to the door, she opened it. "Leave."

"Dr. Pennington, this won't do you any good."

"Oh, yes it will. I'm going to leave town, and then your story will die."

He looked stunned. "I've seen you and Stanton together. The two of you have a thing going. You're not going to leave."

"You don't know me, Mr. Warner. If my leaving will save Nate the attention he doesn't want, then that's what I'll do."

"You're crazy! You could make a fortune from this."

She made a sound, half between a protest and a laugh. "Mr. Warner, you don't have the first clue about what I do, or who I am or where I've come from. A fortune is the last thing that matters to me. I can't believe that a little girl as sweet and good as Jenny could have you for a father!"

That arrow hit its target squarely, and Jack Warner reddened. "You say I don't know you? Well, you don't know me. My parents had nothing. I worked day and night to put myself through college. I'm going to make sure Jenny *has* what she needs."

"If she has your love and support, your time and attention, she won't need anything else," Brooke said with a certainty she knew deep in her soul. She motioned to the door. "Please leave, Mr. Warner. And know that if you write your story and you have it printed in the biggest paper that will buy it, I will be nowhere to be found."

Looking confused for a moment, as if he didn't know what to do or say next, he took a step back. Then, apparently seeing the sheer determination on her face, he turned and left.

Brooke stood rooted to the spot, hearing his footsteps as he descended the stairs. Tears came to her eyes, welled up and overflowed. She wanted to sit down right there on the floor and cry. But she knew she couldn't do that. When Nate got back, she'd have to tell him what happened. She had to pack up her things and Angel's, so they could leave at daybreak. Then she'd have to call Granna and her father, and tell them it would be a few weeks until she could contact them again.

The tears kept flowing, and a sob caught in her chest. But from the strength she'd garnered since she was a child, she closed the door and faced the task ahead.

When Nate pulled up in front of the clinic, he saw the light in Brooke's apartment and switched off the ignition. He was bone tired, but wired, too. He hadn't slept after their return from California. How could he when Brooke had made him an offer that seemed like heaven and hell combined?

Angel, on the seat next to him, meowed from her carrier, and Nate soothed, "You're home now."

Frisco stretched forward and put his paw up on Nate's shoulder from the backseat.

"You know, boy, I thought we had a home when I built that house. Yet if Brooke doesn't share it with us it's going to seem damn empty. Still, how can I make her choose? How can I make her turn away from a light inside of her that she's thinking about capping?''

Frisco and Angel didn't have any answers, and Nate didn't know what he was going to say to Brooke. He wanted her. He felt a deep need for her that he'd never felt for a woman before. Yet needing and wanting couldn't solve their dilemma.

As he carried Angel's carrier, Frisco leaped up the steps quickly and passed him.

After Nate knocked on Brooke's door, he opened it and stepped inside. The chaos he met almost made him take a step back, but Frisco surged ahead of him over to the bed where Brooke was methodically packing clothes in her suitcase. Nate recognized the boxes sitting on the kitchen table as the ones that had carried her dishes and books, the books that had lain on a shelf underneath the coffee table and were now strewn across the sofa. He told himself there was an explanation. He told himself not to jump to conclusions.

To keep from erupting, he lowered Angel's carrier to the sofa and unzipped it. The kitten, who had been so sick a month ago, poked her head out. Seeing familiar surroundings, she jumped over the side of the carrier and ran to Brooke, meowing up at her mistress. Angel was the picture of health now, and Nate still couldn't believe it. There was no sign that she hadn't completely recovered. Her fur was silky and glossy as she looked up at Brooke and meowed again.

The full realization of what was going on around Nate hit him. ''What are you doing?'' It was a stupid question, but one he had to ask.

Tears streaked Brooke's cheeks, and as she looked up at him now he saw the anguish in her eyes. ''I have to leave.''

The words were hardly audible, but he heard them as clearly as if she'd shouted them. He wanted to shout, You can't, I need you! but instead he asked, "Why?"

"Because Jack Warner came here earlier. He...he had been here before...before we went to L.A."

The turmoil inside of Nate spiraled faster. He was very aware of what Jack did for a living. He was even more aware that Brooke had kept this from him. "Why didn't you tell me?"

"It wouldn't have done any good. We were going to L.A. I didn't want to spoil it. I wanted the time with you...to just be with you."

"You know how much I hate secrets."

As tears spilled from her eyes, she apologized shakily. "I'm sorry. I thought everything would be all right. Jenny told him what happened with Biscuit. He thought it would be a great human-interest story. He didn't believe the kink and chiropractor theory any more than you did. But he had no proof, and I told him he was mistaken. We left it at that. He just warned me he'd be watching me closely."

Anger simmered in Nate that Brooke had kept the information from him, that she hadn't come to him, trusted him enough to deal with it with her. "So, why did he come back?"

Brooke sank down on the bed beside the suitcase. "He followed us to L.A."

The full weight of what Brooke had said settled on Nate. "He found out I'm Perry Stanton's son."

"Not only that. He checked into my background and dug up the article about me in the Chicago paper. He knows that what happened with Biscuit happened before, and he thinks he can make his career with this. He doesn't want to be a reporter in Whisper Rock. He wants a byline on some metropolitan newspaper. Nothing I said would budge him, Nate. He's going to combine the stories, talk about how we're involved, reveal who you are.''

"What else did he find out in L.A.?" Nate felt as if everything he'd worked for since he'd left California had vanished into thin air.

"He was in the studio during the telethon, watching us. He saw us hurry away from that meeting with Cole and your parents. That's an angle he's going to play up...that you don't want anything to do with Cole.''

She was openly crying now, and more than anything Nate wanted to hold her. But he couldn't. He was so angry that this had happened, so angry his life was going to be turned upside down again. But most of all angry that Brooke was packing.

"So you're going to run away from it? Leave me here holding the bag?''

Standing, she came so very close to him and shook her head. "No. Don't you see? I *have* to leave. If I stay, the story will go on and on. If I leave, you'll only be in the public eye for a little while, maybe only a day or two. The story won't go national if they can't find me. It'll settle down quickly. If I stay, who knows where Warner could take it? Who knows what you'd have to deal with? I don't want your practice to suffer. I don't want *you* to suffer. I'm going to leave before daybreak.''

Everything inside of him shouted, You can't! Desperately, he tried to reason with her. "You could stay and see what Jack does with this. Maybe no one will care.''

"No one will care that you're Perry Stanton's son? No one will care that you were once a star, too? No one will care that I can seemingly make the impossible happen?''

She was right. And she knew that he knew she was right. There didn't seem to be any other options. If she left, he'd weather the storm and it would only last a week or so. Once everyone in Whisper Rock knew who he was, they'd get used to the idea, and it wouldn't mean a thing. He hoped. But if she stayed...

Turning away from him, she swiped at her tears and continued packing.

"Where will you go?" he asked hoarsely.

"I'm not sure. Maybe up to Colorado. I won't practice for a while. I have some computer skills. I can get a job doing that."

He took her by the arm and swung her around. "That's ridiculous."

She shook her head. "Nate, I'm tired of this. I need peace, too. I need to regroup, get my life in some kind of order. I can't keep moving it over and over." A sob caught in her throat. Pulling away from him she said, "Please go. You're just making this harder."

He knew he was. Yet he couldn't seem to say goodbye. "You have to let me know where you are."

Closing her eyes, she took a deep breath. "What good would that do? You're not going to want your life stirred up again. What would we be? Pen pals?"

Frisco had been sitting and watching them, but now he went over to Brooke and took her hand into his mouth.

"Oh, Frisco." She petted him on the head, then dropped down beside him, bowed her head over him and hugged him.

Nate felt as if he were being torn apart, and he knew he had to get out of here, so he could think straight...so he could figure out what to do.

Standing, Brooke turned her back to him and murmured again, "Please go."

He didn't hesitate this time. When he snapped his fingers at Frisco, the dog came to his side. Angel hopped up on the bed as if to comfort Brooke.

As Nate made the way to his house, his world felt black and void and he just wanted to be alone.

In the yard he said to his dog, "Stay out here and romp around a bit."

Frisco cocked his head and looked at Nate as if he understood, then he took off toward a cottonwood.

After Nate made sure the gate was secure, he went inside the house. The silence beat like an emptiness he'd never known. He'd never felt so much like punching something in his entire life. Not even after the scandal had broken. Not even after Linda had broken their engagement. The idea of Brooke leaving...

As he walked into the living room, he could remember when Brooke and Tessa and Angel had spent the night with him. Everything about it had seemed so right. Everything about Brooke in his life had seemed so right.

Not sure whether he should go for a high-speed drive, take Frisco for an exhausting run or break open a bottle of Jack Daniels, he unzipped his jacket and tossed it over the arm of the recliner.

His doorbell rang.

Hope leaped inside of him. Maybe it was Brooke. Maybe she had decided to stay. Yet why would she stay and face the hullabaloo when he hadn't said he'd stand beside her and support her? The thought suddenly shook him that he'd done to Brooke what Linda had done to him—walked away when life threw a curve. She hadn't told him about Jack Warner because he hadn't given her reason to trust him. How could he walk away from Brooke when...

He loved her.

He'd hardly had time for that insight to register when the doorbell rang again and he hurried to the foyer.

When he opened the door, it wasn't Brooke he found

there but Jack Warner. "What do you want?" Nate snapped. All of his fury and pain focused on the reporter.

"Don't take that attitude with me, Stanton. I've been sitting out there in my car waiting for you to get back from Dr. Pennington's to see if you'd be more cooperative than she was."

Nate wanted to throw the man out on his ear, but he knew that wouldn't solve anything. "I'm not going to cooperate and have you splash our lives all over the newspaper."

"If you'd cooperate, I wouldn't have to splash anything. You could talk about your side of it—not only about your brother and your family, but your reasons for hiring Dr. Pennington. You could work it from two angles. Either you didn't know anything about her background and her special abilities have taken you by surprise, or you knew about the rumors that followed her and you hired her for that reason."

Nate wouldn't use any of this to benefit himself.

His silence wasn't the answer Warner was looking for. "Look, Nate. I don't know if I believe any of this stuff...that Brooke actually healed Biscuit's leg. I mean...that would make her extraordinary. I only believe in what I can see, what science tells me, not in some mystical healing power. But as I tried to explain to her, this story is everything to me."

"It's money to you," Nate said curtly.

Warner pointed his pen at Nate. "It's not like you have to worry about money. Look what you came from. I wasn't so lucky."

Anything Nate had done in his adult life, he'd done on his own. But he wasn't going to try to explain any of that to this man. "If you want to write a story, you're going to do it without my help. And, as far as the story goes, once Brooke's gone you won't have one.''

"Gone? She's really going to leave you?"

"No, she's not leaving me. I left her by walking out when I should have stayed." Could Brooke forgive him for that? Could he convince her that he was worthy of her trust and he would stand beside her?

Nate knew he had said too much to Warner.

All of a sudden, Nate saw a blur of motion and realized it was Frisco running across the clinic's parking lot! Nate swore as he guessed Warner mustn't have fastened the gate securely. A car sped by, and Nate saw why Frisco had taken off. He was barking at the vehicle and trying to catch up to it.

Pushing by Warner, Nate ran outside, calling Frisco's name. But Frisco didn't pay any attention. A second car followed the first. As Nate ran toward his dog, Frisco stopped, turned toward the oncoming car and seemed to freeze. There was the sound of a horn...brakes—

Nate closed his eyes and sucked in a breath as the impact happened, and Frisco lay hurt by the side of the road.

"No," Nate cried as he ran toward his best friend.

The driver of the car that had hit Frisco kept going.

Brooke must have heard the horn and Nate's shout because she came rushing up beside him.

As Brooke knelt by the shoulder of the road, she saw the devastation on Nate's face. She'd heard the blare of the horn, the screech of brakes and then the squeal of tires as the driver left the scene. She'd heard Nate's shout, and she'd known something terrible had happened. Now she watched the man she loved as he felt for Frisco's pulse. The anguish on his face was clear, and she knew what it meant—he thought Frisco was gone.

"Let me feel," she murmured to Nate as she crawled

closer to Frisco and put her hands on his body. She had
never prayed specifically to be able to help an animal.
She'd always accepted the heat and flow of energy when
she could, acknowledging that sometimes it was there and
sometimes it wasn't. But this time was different. This was
Frisco. As her grandmother had taught her, she'd prayed
every day to use her gift the best way she could...to follow the light...to treat every creature, animal or human,
with love.

Now she prayed as she hadn't prayed before. "Please,
let me help Frisco. Please, help me make him whole."

As she gently settled her fingers in his fur, she knew
she might have no choice but to let him go.

Closing her eyes, concentrating, she thought she felt the
flutter of life. Was it her imagination? Was it wishful
thinking? Then she felt it again. It was very weak, but it
was there.

She visualized light flowing into her...and flowing into
Frisco. A healing blue light. A surge of energy passed
through her that almost made her weak, as she held on to
Frisco and let it flow through her hands. The flutter of life
she'd sensed grew stronger.

Leaning down close to him now, she murmured by his
ear, "Come on, boy. Open yourself up to it. Accept it."

The fieriness of the heat in Brooke's hands almost made
her want to pull away. But she knew she couldn't. This
was the gift she'd been blessed with. This was the gift
that she knew now she could never turn away from. This
was the gift that she would never understand but would
accept because she was part of a plan to help the creatures
she loved.

She didn't know how long she crouched over Frisco, passing her hands over him...murmuring to him...hoping...
praying...believing...loving.

Suddenly she felt Frisco's front leg move. She sat back on her heels, her hands still on him.

When his eyes opened, she saw vigorous life there. Her hands were cooling down. The buzz of energy that had fortified the dog was diminishing. It ebbed until she felt weak.

Frisco raised his head and then struggled to his feet.

When Brooke glanced at Nate, she saw the tears in his eyes.

"Are you all right?" Nate asked Brooke hoarsely. "You're so pale."

"I'm fine," she murmured, needing to catch her breath, feeling as if she'd run a marathon, feeling as if her limbs would never be strong again.

Frisco wasn't standing evenly on his front legs and he lifted one as if it hurt. But then he nudged toward Nate and licked his face. Nate put one arm around the dog but was still obviously concerned for Brooke as he asked, "Can you make it to the house?"

She pushed to her feet to prove to him that she was fine. "Yes."

Lifting Frisco into his arms, Nate carried him to the porch, making sure Brooke was beside him, obviously worried about her as much as Frisco. On the porch he set Frisco down, took his hands over the dog and then straightened.

Brooke was leaning against the porch railing when Frisco came to her and sat at her feet. She knew that was his way of thanking her.

As Nate faced her, she wasn't sure what she read on his face until he said, "Don't leave."

Wearily she replied, "You know I have no choice."

"You *do* have a choice. You can't keep running from who you are and what you can do. I've been an idiot,

Brooke. I love you. I love you so much, the thought of you going away leaves an emptiness in me I can't deal with. You were abandoned by your father, you were abandoned by Tim Peabody, and I almost abandoned you, too, by not accepting this wonderful gift of yours...by not accepting who you are. I don't want to live without you, Brooke. I want you to stay. I accept who you are and what you can do. No matter what happens, together we'll face whatever comes our way. Will you marry me?''

All of her life, Brooke wanted this—complete acceptance, a place to belong, a home. She loved Nate with all of her heart. Yet, because she loved him... ''You don't know what you're in for. Your clinic could suffer.''

''I think you're looking at this all wrong. I don't think *you* know what you're in for. I'm the son of Perry Stanton, and anything can happen.''

Stepping closer to her, so close that she could feel his strength, he enfolded her in his arms and looked down at her with more love than she'd ever seen in her lifetime. ''I love you, Brooke. I want you to be my wife. Will you?''

She felt the certainty in Nate that they could, indeed, face anything together. Gazing into his eyes, seeing the extent of his feelings for her, her heart answered the only way it could. ''Yes, I'll marry you.''

Then Nate was kissing her with the fervor of a man who loved deeply and passionately...with the commitment of a man who believed in the strength of bonds...with the love of a man who knew how to make a vow that would last for a lifetime.

She was lost in happiness, Nate's desire, the promise of the future they'd have together, when she heard a cough and then a man clearing his throat.

Nate broke the kiss but kept an arm securely fastened around her as they faced Jack Warner.

With everything that had happened with Frisco, she hadn't even been aware that he was still around. He looked pale and disconcerted.

Looking straight into Brooke's eyes, Warner asked, "Did you do what I think you did?"

Frisco stood at attention beside her as if to protect her, and she patted his head. Something in Jack Warner's demeanor, something in his eyes, told her he wanted to know the truth. And not simply for a newspaper article.

She looked up at Nate, and he gave her shoulder a squeeze. She knew now he would support whatever she said, whatever she decided to do. She told Warner, "Frisco was seriously injured. He was still alive when I put my hands on him. But his injuries healed while I held on to him."

The reporter looked down at Frisco, shifted on his feet and then addressed both her and Nate. "Look. This was just a story before I saw what happened. Now...I don't know what I saw, any more than I know what you did. But whatever happened seemed...important...sacred even. In spite of what you believe, I do have a conscience." He looked at Brooke. "I do want Jenny to look up to me. I don't want to tamper with anything I saw here today. So what I want to know is, are you two willing to compromise?"

"What kind of compromise?" Nate asked.

"I won't dig up Dr. Pennington's past. I won't mention her...special ability. But in return for my silence on that, I want to do a story on you, Nate. I want an in-depth look at what it's like to be Perry Stanton's son. I want to know why you moved here from California after the scandal and how you feel about it, why you turned your back on acting

when you were a kid. I don't just want some glib quotes
or surface material. I want a real interview. If you can
give that to me, I might be able to sell it to one of the
magazines.''

Nate seemed to think about it for a few moments and
then he checked with Brooke. ''What do you think?''

''I think it's up to you,'' she said quietly.

''I'm just coming to terms with all of it,'' he told Warner honestly. ''But if you're willing to be fair, that means
not lifting anything I say out of context, I'll give you the
interview. If you give me a day or two, maybe I can
convince my brother to come out here and do it with me.''

Warner's face lit up. ''Sounds good to me.'' He gave
Nate his business card. ''Call me when you're ready.''
After he stepped down off of Nate's porch, he turned and
asked, ''What are you two going to do if this does get
out?''

Nate answered, ''We won't do anything. The press and
anyone around us can say what they want. Anyone who
comes to Brooke for help or brings pets to our clinic, will
know we're doing the best we can, no matter what methods we use.''

As always, Brooke felt so much admiration for Nate,
for his strength of character and integrity.

After Jack Warner walked away she asked, ''Do you
think we can live a normal life?''

Taking her into his arms again, Nate smiled. ''No life
is normal. We're going to live our life…together.''

Then his lips came down to meet hers again. She was
swept away, thinking only about loving Nate forever.

Epilogue

Christmas Eve, Almost Two Years Later

On Christmas Eve Nate and Brooke's house was full of laughter, chatter, barks and meows. Nate looked around the living room at Cal and Cole trying to set up a train set for Tessa, at his father and Granna discussing the merits of homemade wine, at Tessa reaching on tiptoe to hang an angel ornament on the tree. He realized he'd never been so peaceful, contented or downright happy in his life. When Brooke had suggested both of their families come for Christmas this year, he'd been leery of the idea. But they'd all arrived yesterday, and it seemed to be working out. Granna and Tessa shared one guest bedroom, while Cal slept in the other. Cole had insisted the couch in the living room was fine for him. His mother and father were staying in the apartment over the clinic. And tomorrow Ramón was coming to join them for Christmas dinner.

Nate went to Tessa and lifted her so she could reach

the branch she obviously wanted the angel to hang from. She grinned at him, and he thought about the news he and Brooke were going to share with their families tonight.

As Tessa's feet touched the floor once more, Brooke and his mother came around the corner from the kitchen, both of them carrying trays with cups of eggnog.

"Brooke agrees my recipe for eggnog is the best she's ever tasted," Muriel said proudly.

Brooke's gaze met Nate's. The excitement and startling desire that had overtaken him the first day he'd met her hadn't diminished one iota. In fact, if anything, he desired her more, respected her more, admired her more, loved her more.

She approached him with the tray and held it in front of him. "Mine doesn't have any rum in it," she confided with a wink.

"You can have a taste of the rum when I kiss you," he drawled, and he could see she was as affected by the thought as he was.

"If you're naughty, Santa's not going to visit you tonight," she warned him with a tilt of her head, her dark hair swaying over the turquoise velour, long-sleeved, very sexy jumpsuit.

"All I have to do is look at you in that thing and all of my thoughts become X-rated fantasies."

"Hmm, Dr. Stanton," she said with a pensive look. "We'll have to discuss that problem later...when we're alone."

Glancing around their very full living room, Nate commented in a wry tone, "I'm not sure we're ever going to be alone again."

Frisco chased Angel and a new addition—a striped yellow kitten named Sandy who'd been left on the clinic's doorstep—around the Christmas tree. The two cats seemed to know he was playing a game, and they hid for a moment behind the sofa, then ran over to the dog as if they wanted to do the chase all over again.

"We'll be alone again in a few days," Brooke assured him. "But not for very long." The light in his wife's eyes illuminated Nate's whole world.

"I want to kiss you," he murmured close to her ear, and tickled her earlobe with his tongue.

She laughed and ducked away from him. "Let me get rid of the eggnog first."

Minutes later she was back at his side. Catching her hand, he pulled her with him over in front of the Christmas tree. "Let's make our announcement before my dad guesses. He's been looking at us oddly all night."

"I thought he was just looking at me that way because you told him what I do."

Since the day Nate had asked Brooke to marry him, almost two years ago now, she'd used the miracle of her gift probably about a dozen times. A few of those times, clients who had brought their pets to the clinic had noticed something unusual happening. But Brooke never announced what she was doing, and for the most part pet owners were so thrilled their pets were whole again, they didn't care how it happened. Word got around, though, and they did have a gentleman who was related to someone in Whisper Rock bring his dog to the clinic all the way from Tucson. The little cocker spaniel was shedding much too much and the man was worried. Nothing unusual had happened that day, but Brooke had put the dog on a special diet of vitamins and mineral supplements, and a month later the man had returned, pleased that Buffer was shedding less and seemed to have more energy. Nate knew if there ever was a hubbub about what Brooke did, the owners of all the animals she'd helped would support her, just as he would. She'd carved a place for herself in Whisper Rock, and the community had embraced her.

"Actually, when I told my dad about it last night he seemed to take it all in stride like your dad did. He said he believed anything was possible. So I really don't think that's the reason he's looking at us as he is."

"Whoo-hoo!" sounded the little electric train as it took its first turn around the tree, and Tessa hugged Cal. "It works. You made it work!"

Nate glanced at his wife and saw she was enjoying Tessa's excitement. Brooke said to her dad, "Congratulations! I couldn't have followed those directions."

Cal laughed, his face reddening a little. "Sure you could have. You always could do anything you put your mind to."

This time Brooke's smile grew shy, and Nate was glad to see the growing rapport between her and her father. They were mending fences, just as he and his dad were. Time, with a lot of love and talking, *could* heal.

Pushing himself to his feet from the floor, Cole approached Brooke and Nate. "When are you going to tell us?" he asked with a grin.

"Tell you what?" Nate asked, straight-faced.

"I've gotten to know you better than you think," Cole said. "You and Brooke are always wrapped up in each other. But for the past two days you're inseparable. Besides, I saw Brooke taking those special vitamins this morning."

"Lawyers are too observant," Nate joked, thankful he and Cole were finally on a friendly basis. This relationship would probably take the most time and the most talking, but they were working on it.

"I'll get them ready for you," Cole insisted, always

glad to step into the spotlight. He clapped his hands. "Everyone, we need your attention."

When Nate had approached Cole about doing Jack Warner's interview, the up-and-coming attorney had jumped at the chance. It had gone very well, and Jack had sold the article to a major publication. Six months later he'd taken a job on a magazine based in Denver. Now Nate just shook his head at Cole's sense of drama, accepting it, because he was his brother.

Cole stepped to the side of the Christmas tree, leaving Nate and Brooke in the limelight. This time Nate didn't mind it.

"We have a Christmas gift for all of you," Nate announced.

"A new puppy?" Tessa asked, because that's what she wanted most.

Nate laughed. Little did Tessa know that Santa was picking up a Yorkshire terrier for her tomorrow from a nearby breeder.

"Not exactly," Nate replied with a smile, "but close. Brooke and I are going to have a baby."

"I knew it," Perry Stanton insisted, as everyone else applauded and expressed their congratulations.

There were more hugs than Nate could count, and he saw the look that passed between Brooke and Granna. He knew what it meant.

A short time later, after everyone had settled down with their eggnog again, as well as distributing presents from their piles in different corners of the room, Nate snatched Brooke's hand and pulled her under the mistletoe in the living room doorway. "I think you owe me a kiss," he said, looking down at her with everything that was in his heart.

"I owe you so much more."

He shook his head. "You've given me so much, it'll take a lifetime for me to prove how much I appreciate it."

As tears shimmered in Brooke's eyes, she asked, "If our baby has the same precious gift I do—"

He had known that was what Brooke and Granna were thinking as they'd embraced earlier. "If he or she has it, we'll respect it. And we'll teach our son or daughter how to use it the best way possible. We'll be here, Brooke, to support and cherish and nurture. That's what matters."

When Brooke linked her arms around his neck, she agreed, "That's what matters."

Bending his head, Nate kissed her—a long, deep, loving kiss which told her once again that raising a child together would strengthen their bonds even more...strengthen their commitment...strengthen their love, which would last through eternity. He had found his soul mate, and their hearts would be entwined until the end of time.

* * * * *

Silhouette Romance presents tales of
enchanted love and things beyond explanation
in the heartwarming series

Soulmates

Couples destined for each other are brought
together by the powerful magic of love....

Broken hearts are healed
WITH ONE TOUCH
by Karen Rose Smith (on sale January 2003)

Love comes full circle when
CUPID JONES GETS MARRIED
by DeAnna Talcott (on sale February 2003)

Soulmates

Some things are meant to be....

*Available at
your favorite retail outlet.*

Silhouette®
Where love comes alive™

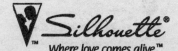

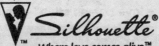

LONE STAR LSCC COUNTRY CLUB EST. 1923

Where Texas society reigns supreme—and appearances are *everything*.

On sale...

June 2002
Stroke of Fortune
Christine Rimmer

July 2002
Texas Rose
Marie Ferrarella

August 2002
The Rebel's Return
Beverly Barton

September 2002
Heartbreaker
Laurie Paige

October 2002
Promised to a Sheik
Carla Cassidy

November 2002
The Quiet Seduction
Dixie Browning

December 2002
An Arranged Marriage
Peggy Moreland

January 2003
The Mercenary
Allison Leigh

February 2003
The Last Bachelor
Judy Christenberry

March 2003
Lone Wolf
Sheri WhiteFeather

April 2003
The Marriage Profile
Metsy Hingle

May 2003
Texas...Now and Forever
Merline Lovelace

Only from

Silhouette®
Where love comes alive™

**Available wherever
Silhouette books are sold.**

Visit us at www.lonestarcountryclub.com   PSLSCCLIST

SILHOUETTE *Romance*

COMING NEXT MONTH

#1642 DUDE RANCH BRIDE—Madeline Baker
Ethan Stormwalker couldn't believe his eyes—the former love of his life
had arrived at his family's ranch in a bridal gown...without a groom! Defy-
ing her father's wishes, Cindy Wagner had fled an arranged marriage. Now
Cindy had to convince Ethan the only marriage she wanted arranged was to
him!

#1643 PRINCESS TAKES A HOLIDAY—Elizabeth Harbison
Princess Teresa of Corsaria wanted a break from the spotlight—she never
intended to be hit by a car! Sexy small-town doctor Dylan Parker kept her
secret while "Tess" healed. But when the truth about her identity came
out, would she choose the royal lifestyle over Dylan's TLC?

#1644 WHAT IF I'M PREGNANT...?—Carla Cassidy
The Pregnancy Test
Unmarried, successful and artificially inseminated, Colette Carson
thought a baby would fulfill her—until Tanner Rothman showed up!
Unsure of her pregnancy—and Tanner's reaction—she kept quiet about
her trip to the sperm bank. But if she *was* pregnant, would Tanner accept
her and another man's child?

#1645 IF THE STICK TURNS PINK...—Carla Cassidy
The Pregnancy Test
Bailey Jenkins was baby-hungry Melanie Watters's best friend—and the
perfect candidate for a father. Although Bailey wasn't interested in being
a dad, he agreed to a temporary marriage of convenience. But when the
stick finally turned pink, would he be able to let Melanie—and his
baby—go?

#1646 CUPID JONES GETS MARRIED—DeAnna Talcott
Soulmates
Cupid Jones had been helping the people of Valentine, Kansas, find true
love for years, but she'd just accidentally matched Burke Riley's mail-
order bride with another man! She volunteered herself as a replacement—
even though she could lose her special gift. Would her own marriage end
her matchmaking days or prove the best match of them all?

#1647 THUNDER IN THE NIGHT—Donna Clayton
The Thunder Clan
Conner Thunder returned to Smoke Valley Reservation to confront his
nightmares, not fall in love with Mattie Russell. But Mattie led a secret
life—a life Conner didn't understand. Now Conner must face his own
secrets in order to keep Mattie in his life—in his arms!—for good.

SRCNM0103